	From Area codes 01923 or 0208:	From the rest of Herts:
Renewals:	01923 471373	01438 737373
Enquiries:	01923 471333	01438 737333
Minicom:	01923 471599	01438 737599

SE

Naor
the c
educa
has l
novel
and i
Mitcl
socia
Argy
had
hies,
histo
Quee
lives

AD SJ

SEA-GREEN RIBBONS

Naomi Mitchison

with illustrations by
BARBARA
ROBERTSON

BALNAIN BOOKS

Back cover photograph of the author by Sally Mitchison

Printed and bound in Britain by BPCC Wheatons of Exeter

Covers printed by Wood Westworth, St Helens.

The publisher gratefully acknowledge subsidy from the Scottish Arts Council towards the publication of this volume

Published in 1991

by Balnain Books.

Druim House, Lochloy Road,

Nairn IV12 5LF

Scotland

British Library Cataloguing in Publication Data:

Mitchison, Naomi 1897-

Sea-green ribbons

I. Title

824.912 [F]

ISBN 1-872557-04-X

FOREWORD

HISTORY jumps at one in glimpses. What is it, we ask, that those people were worrying about, perhaps dying for? And does it mean anything to us now? Are some of them perhaps questions for which there is still no answer? Are they the same old questions that are turning up now, but dressed differently? Can we hear their voices? Where would we have found friends? And, when printed words were beginning, did they mean the same thing as they mean now? Surely not. But yet, the printed words are what stick.

Today there are words around everywhere, radio and telly and always the print, the published words. Are they how we shall be judged by the future? Not ourselves, only those words of ours?

We begin to get into this stream of printed words some three and a half centuries ago; another half century and the stream is coming fast and from more directions. Now we are getting glimpses of how the people who wrote and read these words

must have looked and thought. Moving along the seventeenth century, watching and listening, we get into a crowd, some comfortably dressed, others in rags, all moving, often looking for something to hold onto, sometimes sure they have found it.

To us, looking on, things begin to appear clearly in an uncoiling European world, these three centuries back. We begin to understand one another. Voices and problems, very near, only the wording a little different. People wanting the same things we want: fair shares, security, even happiness, saying openly what we think, getting together, arguing, hunting for the solutions of problems, such as those in the unknown world of science. Look close. The ways of social and political expression are not quite today's, but that doesn't matter. Take their hands – they are talking back.

A book was given to me recently that was once a pamphlet to be handed out in the streets of London, only now it was bound in green leather, the owners' names at the beginning, first Laski, then Brailsford. And now me. In strong letters the book advertised itself against its enemies: *The Tryal of John Lilburne*. So I went sailing off into the mid-seventeenth century in one of those narrow, crammed little streets in central London, with a boiling up of politics, all on the edge of a Christian expression with a new message. It was so exciting that I started to write a play about it, stupidly forgetting that a new play with some twenty or forty characters would never be seen again on the British stage.

But this time, as in *The Oath-Takers*, there was a historian ready not only to accept but also to change the workings of a fiction writer. This was of course Christopher Hill; and our old friend Brailsford would have approved. In history we touch hands. I could no more have written about the seventeenth century without him than I could have written about the eighth without Rosamund MacKitterick.

Of course there were other history books – a good number for the 17th century – many of which I read, and sometimes imagined writing in the shade of, but none would have been the right partners, as these two have been for me. All this is a matter of working together, perhaps dreaming together. Both historians were willing to answer quantities of stupid questions, but perhaps among them, one or two which started an idea.

So now back to the Thames edge, three and a half centuries ago, and crowded, smoky, London bursting out into new beliefs and ideas.

CHAPTER ONE

HOW CAME it that, child as I was, it seemed to me a great thing beyond any expectation when we moved to London?

At first there was little change, but in a while I began to see a new picture. My father had now set up as a printer with one of the new presses from Holland that took away some of the hardest lifting and holding. It seems strange to me that here is a country where we cannot easily speak to one another, but yet we cherish certain goods from there and they the very same with some of ours. We were Protestants together, more comfortable than ever we were with the Scots. They have many printed books in English, so there is understanding between readers. Our neighbour in London, Mr. Overton, had lived in Holland and thought well of it and now indeed there are a sad many of our old friends who have spent years across that small water. So, to return to my family, this new Dutch machine was light enough for my mother, or myself when I was grown a little, to handle it.

There was in all ways a great difference from the old days and our small cottage of one room with a loft above, and wet running down the walls all winter, near Colchester. In London we sat under a new preacher. There were things said which left me at first in a grievous puzzlement. Yet my father seemed to relish them and after a while I began to have a clear understanding of his reasons. But to do this it was needful to think of the years we had lived through, the terrible marching of armies, the day my mother hid herself and me under the hay, out of sight, her hand over my mouth, since even the Parliament soldiers might have wicked thoughts.

At that time my father was only a prentice printer, so that he could not marry. He and my mother were only handfasted, but I cannot believe they sinned, and certainly my father worked all the harder. The printer who was his master seemed mostly to make up small books of sayings or songs. Once, my father told me, he had printed a play, but it seemed there were some lines which might be made to appear as mockery of the Court, so all copies – as luck fell only the first few had been printed – must be destroyed. But much of it was single sheets with the weavers' prices for bay and say – say being the fine cloth, sometimes with silk in it, which was woven in Colchester and the better part of the town's incomings. Even with the war all around them the selling went on and the news came in. Sometimes my father would speak of it, indicating to my mother what things had plainly gone with God's intentions, such as the battle of Marston Moor.

When my father's apprenticeship was over and he found that his savings were enough and he began to have a small business, he married my mother and in God's good time there came a little brother who was more to them than I was. When I turned this over in my mind, as I did when I was old enough to consider such matters, it seemed that they had known that they were sinning, when they got me out of marriage, or at least my father must have known; but that sin was over and the child which had been born now was as it were a token of their re-admission to the chosen of God. I thought, when I began to put my mind to such things, that this might be a kind of Arminianism, since, even when my father was lawlessly getting me on my mother, either he – or for that matter she – was among the saved. Or was not. And deeds could not alter God's sentence on them. But now I know this is folly, and

I am almost shamed to have thought it.

Even at that time I could not put the thoughts I had into words, nor could I have done so without offending my parents. And now it seems to me neither here nor there, although once it seemed real and painful. And I have always tried to follow the Commandments over this as far as in me lay. Be what it may, there was always something unhappy between me and young Stephen. After we came to London there came my little sister Doll and then the others. But indeed I was still young. My father sent both my brother and me to school, but Stephen had more time to play, for I had also to learn the household things that every woman must know. But at least I learned to read and cherish the written word. In London we had coal fires which did not burn out so quick as our old wood firing, but left a sad amount of dust. When the river fogs came they were far away worse because of the coal.

So I grew up in London and made friends with the children of my parents' friends, and also I began to listen to the grown people speaking about events. This came about mostly at the end of the discourse by Mr. Knowles, our Minister and a strong gutsy speaker against all injustice. We waited in the church porch and the men spoke of all that was happening, giving vent to doubts and angers as well as praises, while mothers and children let the wind blow. Yet it seemed to me that much was sent to try our souls and strengthen us against evil, as surely our soldiers had been strengthened at Marston Moor and then at

Naseby. The Scots with their Geneva looks had come and gone, not having convinced the people of England to follow this covenant. Harvests had been poor, yet there had been worse. And also and beyond all – there had been the beheading of the King, here in London.

Dearly would I have liked to be present. I was then a little short of twelve years old and could parrot a dozen sayings against the rule of Kings. Yes, I was mightily pleased to wear the sea-green ribbons which meant that the wearer was against kings and bishops and lords of all kinds. This was the talk I listened to from my corner, when our neighbours, Mr. Overton and Mr. Walwyn, came in. But my mother would not have me go to Whitehall. She herself was afeared of crowds, perhaps, in her heart, of London itself. Once or twice we had been into the great Hall at Westminster, where there was debating or preaching, as well as many sellers of trifles – yes – you could buy a knot of sea-green ribbons there.

You could see all the world's doings. Three times I went to Westminster Hall which seemed like the very middle of England, with my father and brother Stephen. He told us the names of the great folk there; we might even see General Cromwell himself, or Fairfax who had saved Colchester, and many whose names were part of street talk... Members of Parliament, writers, lawyers, as well as many ladies of the Parliament cause in gowns of fine cloth or velvet with a petticoat almost as fine, and white neckerchiefs with perhaps a jewel at the throat.

As my brother grew up, so my father was more apt to take him and leave me to my house tasks, which our mother always had for me. Yet sometimes it was she who took me to our neighbour, Mrs. Elizabeth Lilburne, the wife of Lieut. Colonel Lilburne, who was trying to start up again in trade, but much hampered by the Merchant Adventurers with their monopoly of the wool trade at that time. He was never a true business man, but always dropping his work for politics. There was also Mr. Overton with his great streaky beard and his teeth white as he laughed, who was a printer, for indeed our London street was almost a printers' corner, and there was by now clear understanding that the printed word was stronger than all the swords and pikes of an army.

The old censorships had been swept away, along with other Court interferences of our freedom. The book-seller, Mr. George Thomason, had been for many years making a collection of tracts, broadsides and news sheets printed in London – hundreds each year – but yet was himself, though friendly enough, not deeply moved by any of them. One of our printer neighbours who had been out with the New Model men, had bought from his army money one of the new Dutch presses, bigger than my father's, and had two prentice boys. Sometimes one of them would give me a smudged copy of a song, but my mother was most careful that I gave nothing in return of the kind that would please them most. I might take them a slice of cake, but they must go elsewhere for kisses.

Well I remember sitting on a little stool beside my mother and Mrs. Elizabeth Lilburne telling us of the great adventures and perils she had come through; of her deep love for her husband and he, it seemed of her. She had followed him through all the wars, first when Lord Brooke raised a troop of foot for the City of London. Thus she had run from the King's cavalry break at Edgehill, the babe in her arms, this being Robert, the eldest, and I remember looking at him in wonder after this, for it made him about my own age.

It was mostly Captain Lilburne, as he was then, who had held Prince Rupert's men back at Brentford when they had hoped to seize on London. He himself was taken prisoner and held in the castle of Oxford, where he was accused of high treason with a certain sentence of death, as were all the Parliament men. With the help of another brave wife of a fellow prisoner, Captain Lilburne got through a letter to Elizabeth who rushed to Parliament to lay it before the Speaker. Time being so short, the House could only threaten to execute the Royalist prisoners if theirs were touched, but how to get their letter across to Oxford? It was Elizabeth herself who made the journey, dangerously, and so saved her husband and the other prisoners.

She was then with child, she told my mother, but the babe died. 'I had been too deep in trouble,' she said.

I heard afterwards that Elizabeth, while he was still held in prison, had secured for John a place in London where they could live at their ease, yet he would not accept it, for by now he was Cromwell's man, which seemed at that time to be also the common people's. Even as a child, I could see she longed much for even a short space of peace and hope. She told us of the years after this when her husband, by now a Colonel, searched for a sight of the true England, where those who had fought and suffered for freedom and a fair division of earthly goods had been seduced into setting up a Parliament and powers which were indeed a tyranny... the men who had saved their country from kings and bishops now saw their children dying of hunger. This was how Free-Born John as they named him now, began on the writing of pamphlets that caused such great trouble for the wife he so loved: for when he was prisoned in Newgate she went with him. The Parliament, which was by now totally in the hands of propertied men, even sent men to their house and seized all their goods down to the baby linen she had put by for her lying-in.

And so, said Elizabeth, he could not but hear the crying out of the poor citizens in England. He used the great weapon of printing against the oppressors and many a time they played hide-and-seek with those in authority. And I remember she laughed, almost like a girl getting the better of the boys in a game of tom-tit, and it seemed to me even then that this was because she and her John always had the shelter of one another. And this, I said to myself, is the rose blossom which we, who are God's children, are licensed to take and enjoy.

I began to be aware of something that had surely gone wrong, when there were so many people poor and hungry, not just the rag-tag, but those working at trades. And so it was, though I still had my childish admiration for prancing horses and gilded coaches and soldiers in splendid uniforms. For children cannot see far and I was proud of our house round the corner from Half Moon Alley and our small garden strip, with parsnips and carrots, beans and cabbages and herbs for cooking and medicine. And I was pleased to go with my mother to the market along the Thames-side with the boats coming in from up river with meat and eggs.

But I was frighted when beggars came knocking or shouting at the door. Sometimes they would be wounded soldiers with a permit to beg, banging with their crutches or shouting at the doors; if my parents were out of the house I would not answer the knock. Truly I feared them, but also I looked down on them, since they were the rag-tag while we ourselves were above them, my father paying rates and being a city voter. My mother was mostly at home and busy, as a woman must be, but when she was with child or nursing, I had most of her tasks of sewing and cooking and scrubbing, and also, which was more to my liking, cleaning the type. Sometimes I made up words with them!

On the Sabbath I could wear a clean kerchief

round my neck, and there were godly songs. Once, I remember, my mother whipped me for singing some kind of ballad I had heard in the street. My father whipped my brother Stephen for playing with his top on the Sabbath day – though perhaps that is no worse than grown men playing at soldiers. But I was pleased enough at my brother's disadvantage, and a little later I spied on him and caught him playing with other little boys and told on him.

Punishment. Yes, that was the word; most of all in the time when my father had too little money and too great hopes and wants. God was the punisher of all humankind fallen from Grace, even those counted strong and great among us. In the small church on the edge of Colchester we had sat on hard benches, or knelt on hard stone, and we paid over our tithing pennies, put away every week and not to be touched, even when we needed bread. What did we get from it? Nothing, no comfort. It was an instrument from above forcing us into subservience, not of God but of the so-called Church of England which was brim-packed with Bishops and lords, yes and the King, the man of blood on the top of it.

Forgive me if sometimes I use words of violence, I did not understand in my childhood the church words that flowed over me like foul water. I only knew that my father often muttered against the church, mostly on the Sabbath itself, my mother seeking to hush him. At last this could be thrown off when we came to London and he became what was called a Leveller. There were new words spoken, words of hope and change, aye, great and costly changes to come. There was still a great Divine Punisher, but not of us, no, but of the others whom He would pull down, as we had seen, and break off like a rotten branch from a great apple-tree. My father thought highly of this writing and preaching; it was like a good meal, nourishing and sustaining. Yet few of them had truly suffered for their cause as Mrs. Lilburne and some of the others had done.

After the breaking of bread my father and his friends talked mightily over what had been said or done and sometimes hinted, especially about the Parliament party which had sometimes, he said, put on the clothes back to front of the Royalists. It was true Leveller talk, and there was especially our Mr. Walwyn, whose words seemed to go near the heart. One or another would leap to his feet, having received some kind of vision or voice, a message to the world, a new point to be made or enlarged. This might even be in the street, though more likely in one or two of our nearby taverns and all would speak at once, even the women. Our neighbour, Mr. Overton, might join in and then, even on the Sabbath, he might set the type. He had to be careful, for he did not have a proper licence. He was a great believer in freedom.

Yes, looking back, I see all this and the pleasure of advance and certainty that all of us had. Yet it could happen that the godly words left no meaning for me. If I were to look the least morsel left or right I would become aware of things and people, our neighbours – yes, and their boys; I would find myself caught in vain and foolish imaginings. In this congregation there were often returned soldiers. They were very anxious to join the congregation of Levellers, having suffered the un-levelling of army life, even if the officers might have their green ribbons showing at the neck. There were some who had served under Colonel Lilburne now back at their trades, but not perhaps doing as well as they had hoped and often angry that after all their pains and losses, things were not as they would have hoped.

Above all there was so great a multitude of poor people in London, crowding in from the countryside in hopes that there would be work to be had, but finding little. Harvests had been bad again. There would be women begging with country voices, perhaps trying to sell small useless things – or themselves. My mother might give a piece of bread and hard cheese. It was pitiful and we asked ourselves. What was the Protector and his friends' intent for all these poor? Or did they forget them, as the old barons and bishops and Kings had forgotten?

It was not only poverty and hunger. There was a soldier among our congregation of Levellers. He had been with Cromwell's army in Ireland and had himself done things which now made him sick to his stomach remembering them. He could not see any way in which he could get forgiveness and be relieved of his nightmares, and now he hated

Cromwell and all his officers and would begin to shout and sob, so that my father and others had to restrain him.

From time to time we would go also to the preachings elsewhere, or sometimes just my father, for he and Mr. Overton became more and more dissatisfied with the way the world was going – far from their early hopes. Sometimes they went not to Mr. Knowles but to the Windmill Tavern where there was preaching of a kind and much argument. My father might come back in a black mood and if my mother tried to say words of comfort he would shout at her, even beating her a little for being stupid. She had never learned to read more than a few words. We were right to be troubled, for General Cromwell and his grandees were living in the heart of comfort and pleasuring that was far from the lives of common people. They were never hungry, they had clean linen and warm coats, lined with plush. Their wives' hands were not spoiled with scrubbing and cooking, their collars were of foreign lace. I heard too a sad story of a poor gentlewoman from a Royalist family, (but was that to be accounted on her?) She had lost her husband and all her brothers during the war and had herself been hardly treated. She came to General Cromwell, now the greatest man in all England, with a letter which he, it seems, would have looked at kindly, but one of his new grandees pulled her away, showing no mercy. It was as though, having reached to the high places, he had distanced himself from the people of England.

Who, then, were we ourselves and our families? Colonel and Mrs. Lilburne, their children, Robert and the little ones, Mr. and Mrs. Overton, and his brother-in-law Thomas, the widow Mrs. Barker, Mr. Tew, the stationer, William Browne the book-seller and his silly daughter about my own age, Mr. Hoggerill, Mrs. Katherine Hadley, who had been in prison and churlishly used for the distribution of pamphlets – all these who went together to listen to the Word? We with our thoughts and hopes. Sometimes it came that my father would take me, who was best at listening and remembering, so that I could parrot the very words our Mr. Knowles had spoken on our return, to other Sabbath goers.

I was happy enough to go with him, mostly I fear, because he had favoured me rather than Stephen on this matter. But sometimes I wondered, was even he as truly concerned as others in the Leveller camp? Would he have gone to prison for his beliefs or would he always be one that shouted on the side? Yet I listened well and many fine and worthy words came to my ears and so out at my mouth.

I would prepare myself a little, not only in heart and mind, but I would put on my well-washed kerchief that had a small border of lace, and comb all the tangles out of my hair, which was bright enough. Could be that I thought too much of it, for there were times when I might have wished I could, even for one hour, wear a great hat, like those I had seen among the grandees' ladies. Yes, I fell that far...

But thoughts had come to me and indeed it was likely enough, when words which my mother had let slip, that now I was grown to be almost a woman, it was time they found me a husband.

Truly, I was unsure of how all this came, yet I began to glance about and see eyes on me, and would join in some game for a short time, letting my eyes wander and catch a look that brought a pulse of blood to my cheeks which almost frightened me. Yet I must not even think warm thoughts. My father had a prentice boy who slept in the space under the roof. He would touch my hand or shoulder as he sat down with us for first bread. But I shook him off and at last my father gave him a sound beating, which pleased me well.

Now, in those games which meant a choice of partner, there was one of whom I always had hopes that he would choose me. It was Robert Lilburne, the eldest son; he had hair of such brightness, shoulder length, and was growing almost as tall as his father, much like him, but merrier. Sometimes Colonel Lilburne came with us, he and Robert, when we went to hear a new preacher and to find our hearts stirred with the great thought that all are equal in the sight of God.

So, for a short space, my life seemed happy and abounding in sweet thoughts and thankfulness. But after a height there is more pain in the fall. For it came about that there was a dreadful sickness all through London where we, being as packed as herrings in a basket, could not escape. Those who were afflicted had a terrible hot fever and painful pustules all over the body; one heard the crying as one passed a house quickly. It was worse with children. Two of our little ones died – a girl and a small toddling boy – but also Colonel Lilburne's eldest son, Robert, and his next brother.

I went to the church for Robert's funeral and the preaching of Mr. Knowles, knowing all the time that it was his burial, not our wedding. Many a night I cried for him and still he has a place in my heart. At that time I got no comfort from any preaching and I would wake from sweet dreams into hard truth.

It was about then that I found myself much edified by a woman preacher, Mrs. Attaway. It seemed that she had an understanding of suffering and had words of compassion that a man might be ashamed to allow himself to use. Clearly the spirit was in her and there were times when she would prophesy. What she saw was what I desired to see, since it was a tearing down of privilege and power, and I was in a black mood of tearing. So I was proud that we Levellers had so chosen a woman, since that had never been allowed in the old churches.

It was about this time that we had a servant girl, a poor country thing, half-starved after a bad harvest. It pleased me well for I had less house-work and more time for the press and the type. Then the girl stole a blanket and ran away and was not to be found. But my sister Doll was growing and could take her place.

By now my father was saying that he would find me a husband; it was high time that I stopped my moping and started to give him grandchildren. There were good men enough.

And I began to ask myself, 'What am I alive for, what end should I seek? What had God in store for me, and why?'

One day a man came, not young, and with hard hands and a country voice, who had written something and asked my father to print it. I wondered who this could be, since he did not have the appearance of a writer.

He counted out money carefully; much of it was in pence. I heard that his name was Mr. Winstanley, which at that time meant but little to me, and then he smiled at me suddenly and said, 'Daughter, do you know God?'

Some way I felt that I was constrained to answer this in a serious manner. It was as though he wished to ask me and hear from me in a depth of conviction that was altogether strange. It was as though he himself did, in some way, know God. So I answered him with a question, 'But Sir, which of us can say he – or indeed she – truly knows God?'

'That is well answered,' said Mr. Winstanley. 'But you would wish it?'

I saw my father scowling a little. He said, 'You Diggers make much trouble for yourselves. And maybe for us.'

'I am no trouble maker,' was the answer he gave,

and it seemed to me he had a sweet voice and went on, 'I am only taking one step beyond you Levellers, for most certainly your understanding that all men are equal must expand -' and he lifted up his arms – 'to include the equality of land and crops.' And then he turned to me, 'I do most humbly make an insistence of this equality. And I believe that this is part of God.' I would have wished to speak in warm agreement, but it was not for me.

Yet it came to me that I had heard talk of the Diggers, who came to common land to dig and sow and plant, not for selling, but for their own subsistence, and it was said that they were gentle, poor people, many of them hopeless through stress of war. But armies – even our new Model Army – will trample over a house and garden saying that it is done in a just cause and thus there can be no complaint. Some of the poor Diggers had been soldiers themselves in the battle of Naseby, and many had given free quarters to any Army men and their horses, for all were on the side of Parliament.

So it was that these poor men and women came with a few cows and sheep to a certain rough hill that was common land and made themselves as it were little houses out of wood cut from trees and bushes and turfs or old blankets. They set to and dug the ground which was poor enough, but they were careful of it, digging in dung from their own cows and planting roots and green crop and also, in one corner plot, corn, hoping for their daily bread. They had few furnishings but they had sun and rain in due time and they had their worship.

So they dealt well with the land of England and on the Sabbath they worshipped and sang and were glad enough of England's peace after the bitter drink of war, and that this same England was now a free Commonwealth, with the bondage of kingly power gone for ever. It had been such thinking with us Levellers as well, but that was broken by Colonel Lilburne's arrest by the Government forces, when we saw into the treacherous hearts of our rulers, as also by all that we could not but be aware of in London.

The Lord of the Manor which included this hill, although it was known as common, was a certain Mr. Platt. Now he was a malignant rector, a Presbyterian with his own notions of God's service. He had neither love nor patience towards the poor men and women on the hill and would have them thrown out, their crops trampled and their little huts or houses pulled to the ground. We had heard that this man had been to General Fairfax with a story of trespass. The General had at first shrugged him away, but afterwards sent soldiers, not to harm the poor people, and indeed the soldiers had no wish to hurt. We in London had heard this and how the Diggers were pulled off from their hill, their beasts taken and their crops spoiled, and yet the earth and the bushes were common land and surely should be protected from one man's Norman-like rule. We had also been told of some badness among the Diggers, that they held wives in common and such talk, or that women could choose their own husbands, which is how things sometimes are for older women, rich widows and such, and even so it is done through the pretence of a man.

But this Mr. Winstanley seemed a good citizen of England. He trusted my father to publish his writing well in print and set out the title page with good capitals and borders. So all that day, while I was cooking or scrubbing, I could hear the thump of the press and my father's voice, sometimes angry. He was trying to teach the trade a little to my brother Stephen, who would then do well as a prentice. But Stephen was still young and not too easy with long words, so I would take them from him and myself justify the lines of print.

Later I helped carry out the numbering of leaves and place them properly, for the prentice was often careless over this. Also I checked what Stephen had done, for I had no trust in his ability. Indeed I knew more about the trade than many a prentice. I read the pages as I went and I felt inside me a great softness and concern towards the author Mr. Winstanley and the poor Diggers. Often he would put in a little rhyme or else he would quote from God's word as though he himself had written it. It was while I was at this that my father told me he had found me a husband.

My heart was in my mouth at this and I said nothing. In some way in a corner of my mind, I had still thought of Robert as this, although I knew well that it could never be in this world. I could scarcely hear what my father was telling me, with my mother standing by and approving; it seemed not to make sense. They told me it was a good match and little dowry asked for, seeing I was a clean virgin, able to read and write and figure out money.

'But I shall make him a good present,' said my father, 'when you bear your first son.'

So, I thought, is my life laid out, and not of my doing or wish.

What could I say? Soon enough this man came. He was a well-to-do tradesman, a baker, indeed I had seen his shop. My father had said that he was a Leveller, but it became sadly clear to me that he was only a frequenter of the tavern where the Levellers met, where he would shout along with them but with no true conviction. He brought me some little pies with walnuts and twirls of dough, clever enough, and a great pie for my mother.

'You need to be up early at your trade,' said my father.

'Ah, but I shall have done my best work before then,' said he and gave me a look like a hungry dog.

I knew well what he had in mind, for my father laughed and pinched my cheek, which was blushing. Then the man kissed me on the mouth and seemed as though he would never let go of me. I found afterwards that he had been with whores often enough, but had never had the pleasure that he expected from me and which had to be broken into and ordered for his doings as a husband.

So in a few weeks I was married. I could not even convince my mother of the strong aversion I had to this man. It seemed only a child's foolishness to her. I was to have a gown and matching cap like a grown woman, and she could not understand how little it pleased me. Then I was in a house I did not know, where I was mistress but had no joy of it. The months went by and I did not conceive and I thought to myself that I was glad of that. When my mother questioned me and I told her she began to blame herself for not feeding me on certain plants which, she averred, would settle what a man puts into a woman and form it into a child. She came later with these plants and I promised to cook them, but I threw them out after she had left me.

In those months I learned much about baking and also of bad debts and such. I got myself into trouble with my husband for giving credits to those whom I judged to be honest but were not, or perhaps would have been but that times were hard. Too many started some kind of business which then failed. My heart became hardened and I was never truly sorry for them.

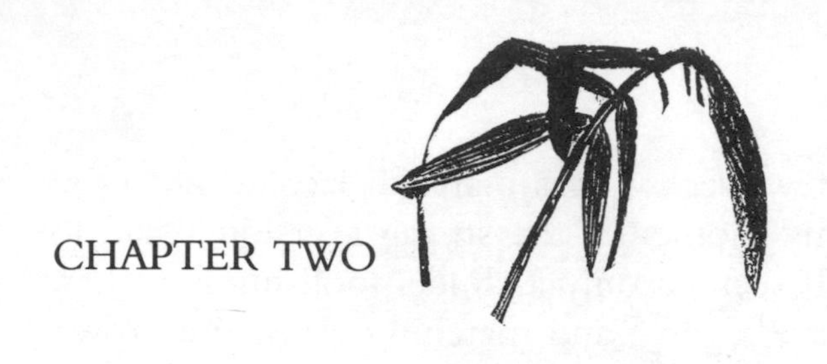

CHAPTER TWO

IT WAS about this time that there was great trouble for the Levellers. The Grandees led by General Cromwell himself turned against us, or so my father and others said,

because they were afraid that those who had been down and ill-treated might rise and do the same thing to others, not only to Cavaliers and Malignants, but even to the topmost officers of the old army whose common soldiers had now been used and then thrown aside. And this was in a way true because there was deep anger boiling amongst the common people of London who felt themselved betrayed. Yet I do not think that even so they would have marched with sword and brand against Westminster, even though they might speak of it when the wind blew.

There was great bitterness of heart then, and Colonel Lilburne was taken off to the Tower of London and Elizabeth left in hot anger going about speaking with all who had known him. And they dared not lay a hand on her. Truly it was astonishing for me to see a woman so well putting A after B and the men listening to her quietly and with respect.

At this same time there were other pamphlets from Mr. Winstanley and persons of his way of thinking. It seemed that Mr. Winstanley and his Diggers were constantly in trouble with those who claimed ownership of the common land, and he wrote of ancient days before the Norman Conquest when land was more justly parcelled out, so that none starved. I wondered if this could have been true. I had no money of my own, only for the housekeeping, so my father, who might have been a little sorry for me, gave me smudged copies, as did Mr. Overton.

There was a different kind of censorship now, not so harsh, but difficult to track down where it might strike. It was clear that some of the grandees held zealously to their position and might be offended. I did not ask Mrs. Lilburne for pamphlets. It hurt me for a long time even to pass close to her house which was too full of painful memories.

My husband gave me good clothes, indeed I had a

coat of say cloth for cold days which turned my thoughts back to Colchester and my childhood. We kept Sabbath but with a preacher who had little to say on what it was my wish to hear. My heart was never lifted and indeed my husband was no true Leveller, as my father had wrongly told me he was, but it seemed to me he judged a man's merit on whether he had money for cakes or only for bread. He might go sometimes to a Leveller gathering, for he liked to be in company and shout with others. Maybe he did not find me as jolly a wife as he had hoped, certainly he was unanxious to have any talk with me on political issues and happenings, or even on matters of the soul, even on the Sabbath and after prayer. He said it was enough if he asked blessing for the meal, hoping the meat was well savoured.

I asked him, might I continue to sit under Mrs. Attaway who preached in her own house. He agreed, but with a degree of disparagement, so that I had little comfort. Sometimes I thought of that kindly man, Mr. Winstanley, and wondered whether he was well or ill, and how his Diggers had fared in the end, for, although they had been chased off St. George's Hill, yet they had gone elsewhere, some this way and some that.

Meanwhile it seemed more and more that the Generals were forgetting that for which they had fought with such courage, and for which England was looking to them. It seemed that having power also meant giving room to the Evil One. Yet General Cromwell himself was, I thought, still a man of

God.

I listened much to talk and at last I took heart to visit Mrs. Lilburne. She was sadly cast down. Yet it was good that Colonel Lilburne after his trial and vindication by the people of London was busy with a new project, soap-boiling, with less time for mourning, the more so as he was never inclined to business and would easily slip into debt and then become angered at how things had turned out.

Indeed my father was busy with his printing, for the people of England seemed to be buzzing with thoughts and images, which they must, willynilly, write down, either in prose or in verse and often in such a way that the true meaning was half-hidden by the ingenuity of the words. But Mrs. Lilburne knew, and I knew, that even if we spoke only of public events, each of us was thinking about the boy Robert and could not be comforted. She understood that my marriage had brought me nothing but heart-break.

We had all been deeply troubled and anxious when Colonel Lilburne was taken from the Tower to be tried, since the powers that were now over us looked jealously at the Levellers and all who understood that people should be equal and not one above the other. But the jury stood by Colonel Lilburne even against what the judges wished, for they respected and honoured him beyond any of the grandees and they seemed to represent the will of London against those who held green lands in the countryside. Now this is all set down in a book which my father printed and which was bought and read throughout England, and words from it would slip into the mouths of preachers for the greater edification of those who were of the same mind. Colonel Lilburne had made in it the most remarkable defence and the breath of God was surely in him to the discomfiture of his enemies. Yet I could not truly rejoice, and Mrs. Elizabeth Lilburne would break off from praising him because of tears. And so it went.

Those who come to visit a printer are more lively company than those who visit a baker, and I longed sometimes for the heady Leveller talk, even though I myself, only a woman and young, would never dare join it, yet the words which I might have spoken ran like mice through my head. I had my sea-green ribbons knotted and hidden under my kerchiefs and the sticks of dry lavender... and I hated to talk agreeably with some of the customers who upheld the power and pleasures of riches, for even if they were not truly rich like some I had seen in Westminster Hall in the old days, they put on airs which they thought would cause them to seem so.

Some of them sent servants to buy bread and sweetmeats for their masters, and sometimes I would give these a broken pie or a piece from a broken cake. But if my husband saw this he was displeased and would make me suffer a little, both by beating and by harsh words, pointing out my barreness, which I was half shamed about, but which also gave me some satisfaction, for it was no child of his that I would want to bear.

Often enough my husband left me in the evening, with a surly word or two, to drink and gossip with those of a like mind and perhaps find an easy woman to enjoy. It was not my place to question or to show anger and indeed, although in some way I was mortified, it seemed better this way than when he stayed in and grumbled at me for being what I was. If he left me early I would sometimes take myself out and wander a little through the nearer streets of London, wearing my plainest coats and kerchiefs and a dark cap on my head, thus making sure that I was not taken for a loose woman.

Sometimes I went into a little dark church a few streets away and which I had avoided earlier, since the congregation appeared to me as unfriends who still clung to the rule of Bishops and such, making me feel I must leap to my feet and condemn them. At least this church was quiet. There was nobody blaming me. At first I had been scandalised by the gilded altar and the paintings on the wall, which seemed to me near Papist, but they took my mind off the life of every day in which there was no colour. It was the same with the little bright windows, though some had been broken since they offended against the direct word of the Lord, taking the looker into a wandering desire.

Here it was that I met a woman praying, who afterwards spoke to me, asking if I had come for the Service, adding that it had given her great joy and comfort – 'in these bad days.'

I looked at her with attention, and it seemed to me that she must be the wife of a Cavalier, or at least the widow of one since she wore dark woollens and a plain kerchief. I felt sorrow for her but I was afraid to answer her kindly, since she might then suppose that I was a member of this so-called Church of England, which I held in little esteem. So, after a few words I turned away, although as I think now, I should at least have taken her into kindly argument.

I began to ask myself, are these coloured pictures and windows, or indeed the altar, forcing itself frowardly into view, as soaked in wickedness as we would have it? Might they not be merely the framing and devices that a well-skilled printer will use to beautify his title page?

Indeed, I felt drawn to go back into this little church once more, but I put it from me. I went instead to hear the woman preacher, Mrs Attaway, but in her stead was yet another woman who had great strength and warmth of spirit and who spoke pure Leveller doctrine. She took it as far as to say that not only was Adam – the poor man with no belongings – the equal of lords and Generals, but also that his wife Eve, whose only dress was of leaves, was a better vessel for God's word than all the bejewelled and silk-coated ladies. This, she said, was Reason – the knowledge and pouring in of truth and light.

This shook me, but I could not totally go with her, for it was against all that I had been taught and grown up with. Yet as I turned it over in my mind I found it had a sweet savour, though not to all the congregation, some of whom had laughed and one had even thrown a stone and spat towards her. This angered me, as also the lewd sayings which I could not but overhear. I thought to myself, who are they to cast a stone, and she, I am certain, a chaste and courageous woman? But I knew with sorrow that what these men were saying would also be in my husband's mind, and I did not speak to him about this woman preacher, for I could guess only too well what he would say. And I wondered about her, whether she had a husband, or perhaps a father, and, if so, what they might say to her. If they were true Levellers perhaps they could accept it and praise her, though I doubted if my father would have done so, and surely never my husband.

So it came about that I went once more to the little church, saying to myself that I must come to an understanding of why a few such churches still remained, for it was far from the thinking of London as I knew it. I felt that going there was a kind of challenge and I tried to anger myself over all I saw for it seemed to be like popery. But there, in the same place, was the lady I had spoken with and when we had greeted one another she said, smiling, would I come home with her.

Now I had been turning over in my mind the sadness and hurt that seemed to be with me all the time, and this seemed like a small break, so I went with her to some lodgings in a large old house. I asked, did she live alone?

'With my brother and sister-in-law' she said. 'My husband – this terrible war.'

So it was clear that she was, as I had thought, a widow. It was a strange thing, for I scarcely knew her and yet I felt drawn to her. She asked my name and when I said Sarah – for I did not care to give my husband's name – she smiled and said, 'I too have a Bible name. I am Deborah.'

So we chatted a little, cautiously; she gave me a drink of coffee, which was my first, it had a noble scent and I was curious to try it. The cup was fine chinaware but she herself wore an oldish dress and only one small cameo brooch. After a time I was moved to question her gently about her widowhood, so that she began to speak of her husband.

'He did not wish to fight his own countrymen,' she said, 'and the same holds for the other side, surely. I cannot think that they wished to murder their king and have that blood on their hands.'

I could have answered, and that with hard words, but waited, and she went on, almost as though to herself. 'It is said that these things could be sent to punish us for our sins, but I will not agree to that for our lives together were beautiful and surely God loves beauty. My husband was a poet.'

And then she began to speak low, as it were past me, as sometimes one speaks to a friend imagined, as I had indeed spoken low to my own remembrances of Robert, or as sometimes one imagines oneself complaining even to the Lord. Yet I thought that surely she was speaking to her dead husband, this poet, who was a Malignant and an enemy and whom she had loved. Perhaps he had written poems about her. She became silent. What could I say?

At last I asked, as gently as I could, 'Were his poems perhaps published?' For I thought this might break her sorrow a little.

She rose and went to a shelf and took down a small, elegant book. 'Do you care for poetry, Sarah?' she asked.

'I do indeed,' I said, 'and above all when it is as well set-up as this.' For it was most delightfully set up and the type was truly agreeable. I am no judge of verse, but I could see that the man who had written these verses was a scholar who knew his classics.

She smiled a little. 'At least you care for books,' she said. I told her that my father was a printer and indeed I had some little knowledge of the trade.

So then she was quiet for a time but at last she spoke. 'Tell me, Sarah, what is it that brings you to speak with me? Do you often go to that church?'

I did not know what to say. I might say too much. In the end I said, 'I am in a certain trouble.'

'Which perhaps I can help you to mend?' she asked.

Now, either I should say all or nothing. But she smiled at me sweetly, and I found myself telling her of my unhappy marriage which seemed to have ended in a mutual hatred, so that it must surely be better for us to be parted. I knew that a woman must be patient and obey, but it had gone beyond that. And I had the intention – though I had never before put it into words – of leaving him and walking out of London into the country and perhaps hire myself to a baker, since I knew the trade, or perhaps by great good fortune, to a printer.

In my mind, (but I could not say so to this lady, the widow of a Cavalier poet) I truly hoped to find the Diggers, for I had heard that there were some within two day's walk of London, although Mr. Winstanley was elsewhere. If once I found them, I said to myself, I would do any kind of work.

Suddenly I saw the lady Deborah's eyes fill with tears, and it came to me that she and her husband had loved deeply and she had been much hurt. I said timidly, 'Does not the Lord God comfort you a little?'

She sighed, 'That was how we met, you and I, Sarah. But the comfort is – not great.' But she smiled at me, and then, 'You yourself will seldom go to my church?'

'No,' I said quietly. 'My comfort is elsewhere.' I felt I should try to show her other ways. And yet I could not see how she could receive any comfort from the preaching that I most cared for. And this is a strange thing, for surely God's truth should be comforting for all? Must we suppose, then, that truth has two sides?

Suddenly the lady Deborah roused herself, saying, 'I will give you a letter to the father of the man who printed my husband's poems. He himself was a printer and I understand he still may print a few ballads and such. At least he may give you some harbouring. He lives in Cobham, not more than twelve or fifteen miles from London. He is a decent old man, and you will be safe with him. Wait, Sarah, while I write.'

I said, 'God be with you for your great kindness.' I watched her write and I began to wonder what I had done. For although I had thought of leaving my husband and all the pain of our life together, it had only been a thought. Now I had put it into words and it had become real. And also, it came to me, that I had heard of Cobham as a place where some of the Diggers were settled.

Hurrying back lest he should ask me where I had been, I turned all this over in my mind. I asked myself, should I also ask counsel of the woman preacher? But what might she say? Could it be, I wondered, that she would tell me my duty was to my husband to turn him to better ways? Yet that would leave me with something so downright impossible that it could not be. At best he would laugh, at worst it would be the belt or the dog whip. He had used both on me.

So I crept in cautiously and made the supper. I hid the letter well, under the flour in the great crock, and prayed long before I slept. I was troubled in my mind and my thoughts went swirling through me, so that the next day I made a small slip in summing what a customer should pay, a matter of only a few pence, but when he noted it, my husband became angry and called me by cruel names, most of all that I was barren through no fault of his, for he had already let slip that he had a child by one of the whores he had been in company with. His words were so sore that I felt I would almost rather the buckle of the belt.

I could go back to my parents, he said, and see what they had to say. And I thought bitterly of my father's anger and my mother's whining and weeping. So I said nothing and in bed that night he used his hot strength to hurt and punish me.

And so it came about that I took my Bible and the letter to the old printer in Cobham, which I put into the neck of my bodice. I also took what little money I had, a change of linen and a loaf of bread in a wicker basket, but I left behind me the pamphlets, since the best part of them I knew by heart. And, in the morning, when he was baking and sometimes shouting at me, calling me by dirty names, I lifted the latch quietly and set out towards the countryside, out of London for the first time since I was a child.

CHAPTER THREE

IF YOU walk straight on, not looking around, you may well not be molested nor questioned. It is only when you waver that things go badly, that is to say that a journey on earth is like a Journey towards God. So I did not allow myself to waver.

I went on by-ways past St Paul's, since it was there that the printers and publishers forgathered in the church yard, and also I avoided Fleet Street with its nonsenses of entertainments and trivialities. I kept instead near the river, over the small bridges that crossed the dirty streams and ditches with their foul smell of rotting leaves and worse things, then on past Westminster. Here were many Parliament people going in and out of Westminster Hall, some with faces I knew, but none that knew me. Then came the earth dyke that the citizens of London had raised against the Malignant force, but now it was mostly flattened and there was a donkey grazing along it.

I was now out of the city and I knew that I had left my hurt and fear behind me. I even sang a little when the road was clear, as often it was once I had put Westminster behind me. I thought to myself, I must go south and west, making for the Portsmouth road, and I watched the sun. I had my basket under my thick cloak; besides the bread I had taken a few winter apples that were still left and I found myself thinking, He will not be able to make apple pies with these!

It was, as I remember, early Spring and I was astonished at all the green grass and the trees in leaf. I sat down on a bank with small flowers which I did not know by name but half remembered from my childhood. The winter wheat was coming well and there were birds hopping and scratching, bigger and wilder than our London sparrows. Once or twice someone would give me a good morning and I would answer God be with you, but for a long time I walked by the sun and I was not tired because it seemed to me that the Lord had compassion on me and would surely lead me. And my trust was in Him.

Now there were villages here and there, such as Chelsea, often with some great house and churches, but I went past without stopping. Later, as I rested by the roadside there came a man with a cart who called down, offering me a lift. As there was an oldish woman with a hood over white hair I felt safe to accept and indeed the Lord had guided my steps, for the man was an old soldier from Cromwell's army, now retired with a stiff leg and no great cheer over the way things were shaping. His mother was with him and they were set for Putney on the river Thames, where he had a brother in the brewing trade. He had some sacks of barley in the cart, on which his mother and I sat in fair comfort.

When I heard the name Putney I thought at once of the great meeting there at which Colonel Rainsborough and with him, Private Sexby, had been so illuminated by the Lord in their love and concern for the poor of England that they had spoken for them even against the great ones, Cromwell and Ireton.

I spoke of this a little timidly, but both the man and his mother seemed truly of the same mind, for the man himself, who told me that his name was Parret, had been a Corporal and had been at that very occasion when all seemed set for the people of England. It rung in his ears yet, that the poorest that is in England hath a life to live, even as the greatest. Aye, that was it. But what had gone wrong? And why? For none of it had come about and instead there were more lords and turned clergy as bad as the old Bishops. He spoke half to me and his mother but half to himself, his voice dropping.

It was now turning dusk and I was asking myself should I push on towards Cobham, risking the night? But the Lord was surely showing mercy, for my companions asked would I stay the night with them at the brother's house. For a moment I was doubtful, but when the mother, seeing this, offered to share her bed with me, I thanked them and was glad of it. The house smelt strong of ale and there were some rats about, but the old woman and I put up a prayer, spoke a little, and then slept. I had told them my name was Sarah Werden, going back to my father's name. I would never any more think of myself by my husband's name. I woke clear in my mind on that and other things.

In the morning there was a pitcher of skim milk, some thin beer and a poor kind of bread, yet eaten with blessing. And so I set out from Putney on a fine morning and picturing to myself how it must have looked when the army came in, strong and determined and under blessing. How is it that the worst always comes to the top, as bubbles come up through milk boiling and burst? For Ireton flourishes and Cromwell rules our land. But Rainsborough who should have led us, was smitten down. Dead by treachery. And I wept a little thinking of all this.

My thoughts then turned to Mr. Winstanley and his pamphlets which I had read with such eagerness and cleansing of the soul. It seemed that he had been in direct communication with that Christ whom he called Reason, since goodness was so clear and easy once the mind centred upon it, as also was the badness of a non-paradise where Cain had riches and land and all pleasures of flesh and eye, but Abel had nothing beyond the deeper pleasure of the soul that knows God.

Painfully I questioned myself on where did I stand? For it seemed to me that my husband, even when he had drunk and was in the mood, shouting with the Levellers, was still on the wrong side. What truly led him was the shine and clink of money. And if I had stayed as an obedient wife, he would have pulled me with him into the pit.

Yet, was I right to leave him? Should I not have wrestled with him, persuaded him? But how? Had not men and women suffered before, yes surely, their ears cut, their backs beaten and bleeding at the cart tail, but they had neither flinched nor complained, although they were in sorer pain than ever I had. And women also. I minded that my mother had scarcely cried out in the pain of childbirth. And was not that because of the great blessing coming to her afterwards, to wit a new human soul? Yes, but my pain, which was a woman's pain, bore no fruit.

If I had borne a child to Robert, would not my pain have been a kind of joy? Was not a woman's pain, perhaps, part of her inheritance from Eve, for her disobedience? But no, I reasoned, it is not pain itself, but what goes with the pain. I knew, among my own friends and neighbours, of beating by husbands, but little made of it, when all was well after and no bitterness left. While for me it had been bitterness all through, even from my wedding night.

So I trudged on, my feet hurting a little. It was the Portsmouth road and traffic not scarce, but I did not care to take even a little help from any of those who called to me. I mistrusted them, even as I mistrusted my own thinking. There were spring flowers coming at each side of the road, bright flowers like those sold for ha'pence a bunch in the streets of London.

A few miles on there was a small stream running at the side of the road. I stopped to watch some milk cows driven down to drink with two ragged boys herding them. I wondered where this milk was marketed. A little further on and there was a pool with tall rushes growing round it. There was no-one about, so I went down and washed, rubbing myself with green leaves to rid my hands and feet of the grime and coal smell of London.

I stayed a while on the bank, even singing a little and from the bottom of my soul praising God for his green and beautiful creations. Yet, from there I turned to accusing myself of cowardice and lack of faith, for surely there would be punishment coming. Now, the birds and the flowers seemed to be mocking me.

It was in sore distress of spirit then that I came into Cobham and felt under the knot of my kerchief for the letter to the old printer. I asked timidly of a market woman and she pointed down a small alley. I walked through it and along another small street and

I asked myself would I some day get to know it as well as I knew the streets of London, that is the streets around Half Moon Alley and down to the Thames mud edge. I turned off into another street, as she said I should and at the end of it there seemed to be a small hill rising a little way off and I asked myself could that be a sign of my upward going, and I knocked on the door of the house that had the right name painted over it.

I was so abashed that I could not even bear to watch as I gave the letter over to what seemed to me an old grey-beard. I felt in my mind that there was nothing I could do but go back and pray my husband for forgiveness or else throw myself into the river.

The old man lifted his eyes on me, scowling a little, then said, 'Come in,' and held the door open. And then he pointed and said, 'What is that?'

I said timidly that it was a press of the old kind and, following his fingers, I named the fount and the batten and came on to the type case. He threw down a handful of type and asked me what it was. I said I thought it was English Roman No 1 lower face, which is a common type. He nodded and held out another, which was small Pica, which I have never liked setting.

'Find me a kernel letter,' he said and I picked out an f, though I was aware that in some types there are more.

'Which capital goes with the pica?' he asked.

I looked for one in the type case but then said, unhappily, 'There is none in the right place'.

The old man grinned and said, 'You have come in the nick, just as the angel came to Jacob, and now see if you can make out what is jamming this old press, for God help me, my eyes are not what they were.'

I did my best and at last saw what was fouling the slide for the form and picked up the small hammer. He looked at me for quite a while. 'Well,' he said, 'You might suit me better than my rascally prentice boy who went off with the money box, devil take him!'

'Oh no!' I said, shamed that anyone who had to do with this great trade had used it so foully.

'Ah,' he said, 'but luck was on my side.' And then he laughed into his beard.

I only found out many days later when he told me that he had just taken out the good money from the box and there were only pennies left to rattle.

He said, 'You can be my prentice for a while. I have one long and stupid ballad to print and sell to as many fools as will buy it.'

I was out of breath with relief and astonishment at how things were falling out for me.

He went on, 'You had best not look too close at the meaning of the rhymes, since it is not meant for young maids or young wives neither, but for randy old men such as myself.' And then, when he saw me flinch a little he added, 'Ah, but we are worse on paper than in life. So you shall bed in the prentice room where my legs are too old to follow and you will work for me as long as I am satisfied.'

So it seemed that God had mercy on me after all and that I was, as it were, in harbour. And so the weeks went by in Cobham. He believed in the story that was in the letter and did not question me more than a little. I slept in the prentice loft, climbing a ladder, and in time I washed all the blankets and did the same for the old man, Mr. Yates.

Soon enough I was doing the cooking as well. He had been buying bread, not of the best, so I asked him to let me buy flour and I would do better for both of us for less money. Once I made him a bacon pie, which pleased him mightily. And I set the verses, which were dirty enough but I did not allow myself to take in the meaning of them and if any of our customers tried to joke with me, Mr. Yates bade them hold their filthy tongues.

After a while he gave me a little money for myself. I bought some cloth for a new apron and a change of linen. Over my shift I wore a good bodice and one or two petticoats, besides my apron which I washed often and my white linen collar. I had also a good linen cap. We sat together in the evenings and I would patch his shirts.

Sometimes he spoke of his son who had printed that book of poems which I had so much admired. But he himself had not read the text though he had handled the book and approved the title page. He was not concerned over the poet, still less his widow. I was never to know what that old man had in his mind. Perhaps little or perhaps much but clogged over.

I kept wondering could there anywhere be an advertisement for a runaway wife, but if there was, nobody pointed at me. Or again, had my old friend taken notice of it, I do not think he would have considered sending me back.

On the Sabbath day I went to the church with him but was never much edified by the sermon. It seemed to me that the preaching had no fire behind it and there was little discussion after it. And then one day, someone pointed up the street to the small hill one could see with a tangle of bushes and what appeared to be some ploughed land with a crop coming, for now it was into summer. Then there was talk and some laughing, not of the kindest, and I overheard some of them saying that there were Diggers up there, and with no friendly words but much laughter and dirty joking, so that I turned my back away from them. Yet it set me wondering what had happened to that gentle and friendly man, Mr. Winstanley. Some day, I said to myself, I will arise and go up and into the hills.

I heard talk also of how Colonel Lilburne had offered the Government to take his followers to found a colony in the Americas. I wished to my heart that I could have joined them, but how could I make any touch without my family knowing of it? For that, above all, must never be, even though I sometimes dreamed of my mother and more often of one, in particular, of my little sisters. And in the end, it seemed, the offer from Colonel Lilburne was not taken up by the Government. Could it be that they were afraid to harbour a brood of critics far away?

And always there was the talk about General Cromwell, for sometimes he would be as one inspired by God, seeing deep into the divine purpose and how this was manifesting itself in England. Sometimes also he would shout and turn on Levellers and Ranters and indeed on all who did not instantly fall in with his intentions. So which of the faces of General Cromwell, who had meant so much to us, showed to the people of England, was truly his? That was too hard a puzzle for me, and my old master Mr. Yates only laughed when I spoke of it, asking for his opinion, since to him I was only a woman. But I began to think that the common people must fend for themselves and trust no leader, but keep their own freedom, as Mr. Winstanley had shown was open to all.

By now I had become slight friends with one or two young women in the same kind of situation as myself. There was one called Lucy Murren who was apprenticed to a glove maker. She did the heavy embroidery, sometimes even with gold thread, on the backs of riding gloves for the quality and also for high ranks in the army. She would have spent every penny she made on sweetmeats, but I dissuaded her a little, partly by telling her what bad things were often put into cakes and pies, pretending to be honey-sweet but in the end of ill digestion. There was true sugar coming in from the Americas, but this cost more, and not all bakers and pastry makers were truly honest. I knew too well that sometimes my husband had abused his customers over this, although he was not so bad as some. Once or twice, when Lucy and I were together, we would follow a piper for a little dance, hand in hand, keeping ourselves well away from the prentice boys and such.

On market day my old Mr. Yates would send me off to see what was there. He liked fish, easier on old teeth than meat, and we were not too far from the sea. I would listen to scraps of news. It seemed that there was little change in the old Parliament almost at the command of General Cromwell and I asked myself had so many good men died for nothing and must this always be so as a kind of punishment for the follies of mankind. Back in London the Levellers had been put down. I heard the names of some who had been much spoken about and praised yet now, it seemed, were in the dumps. I was glad indeed that my father's name was not among them, as it could well have been, seeing that he had printed works by Mr. Winstanley and others who were now sadly out of fashion.

The year turned to autumn and then winter. I was most vexed to hear that Colonel Lilburne was in trouble again, indeed seemed to be seeking it, and worse than any before. It was death held in front of him now; they were tired of having him putting them in the wrong, most of all those he had helped in other days. As always, the rumour was that Elizabeth was going to all lengths to help him, wearing herself out. How I wished I could have stood by and helped her, as I could have done if only I had been her daughter-in-law as I had so longed to be. Why does everything go so wrong? Who – what – was to blame?

But I had my old Mr. Yates to look after and cosset as far as I could, through the cold days. There was merry-making at New Year, but I did not join in. He seemed to get a little better after that. The days went by and soon it was Spring: I remember the primroses beginning to show along the hedgerows. If there was any small order of printing to be done I did it and Mr. Yates was pleased enough. Some of the type was getting badly worn and I had to be careful especially with some of the capitals. So I was kept busy and only found time after work to question and often to fall into some kind of despair, for what kind of judgement was falling upon ourselves and the land of England?

What I could not fathom, though I sweated over it, was God's intention. Was it perhaps that we had flown too high, had counted on favour from Above, not admitting that all men and women, ourselves included, had fallen from grace? Only, how was I to fit this in with that other picture of God's dear love? And then I bethought me of Mr. Winstanley saying that Christ fulfilled himself in man as Reason. Could he mean, then, that he did not think of God as being outside man? I was greatly troubled, the more so as I had felt a little drawn towards the Diggers.

And then my old man died. I came in from the market one day and found him lying back with his face twisted and not able to speak. I put a pillow behind him and hurried out for the doctor who had been in the house once before. He bled my poor friend, but could give him no help, nor could he even interpret the words he was trying to say. Mr. Yates could not eat and though I tried him with bread sopped in milk he could barely swallow. I could only be glad for his comfort when at last he died. I had sent a messenger for his son, who came only in time to close his father's eyes.

Also I had gone at once to the church when it was clear from what the doctor had told me, that my kind employer had little time left. But I could not tell if he truly heard the words of comfort from the Minister, for he only tightened his grip on me with his left hand, and his right hand seemed to be already dead. But a woman came and helped me to lay him out, so that he had a peaceful look before his son came.

So now there had to be a sad burial, and I myself was perhaps the one that cared the most. The grave was dug, his body laid into it, but I believe I was the only one weeping. I had borrowed a black cloak from one of the neighbours, for it seemed only right that I should be there for the last of him. I got no comfort from the service and was only anxious for myself and what must I do now.

I had half-hoped that, as I had some little skill in printing, the son, young Mr. Yates, might offer me a place. I would have been most happy to learn from a better printer. But he did not. He barely spoke to me, thinking perhaps that I had neglected my old master. In the end he gave me a little money and thanked me coldly. He told me he was selling the house, so now I must fend for myself.

I felt sadly hurt, but I could not say anything to this man. There seemed to be no good way for me to go. So in this manner it came about that I set my face to the hills beyond Cobham with a deep intention to go to the Diggers. I had already made up my mind that by now they were the only ones who stood firm for the rights of the common folk against their new masters.

Lucy had come to stand with me at the burial, with her arm round my neck when I was in tears. But when I told her of my intention to go to the Diggers she was clean affrighted and began to tell tales of them which I could not believe. She said it had been told her that there was no young woman left on the Diggers' hill that was yet a maid and the men there allowed every kind of licence with no reprimand. But that was never what I had found in the reading of Mr Winstanley's pamphlets, when he had spoken on the spirit of reason being found in both men and women, both the sons and the daughters being those who had accepted the doctrines of love. But this love was, surely, not men's lies to get their pleasure, but a deeper thing, part of freedom. The true freedom of the great Creator. I tried my best to explain all this to Lucy, but she left in tears when she saw my determination. And so once more I set out on a journey whose end I could not see.

CHAPTER FOUR

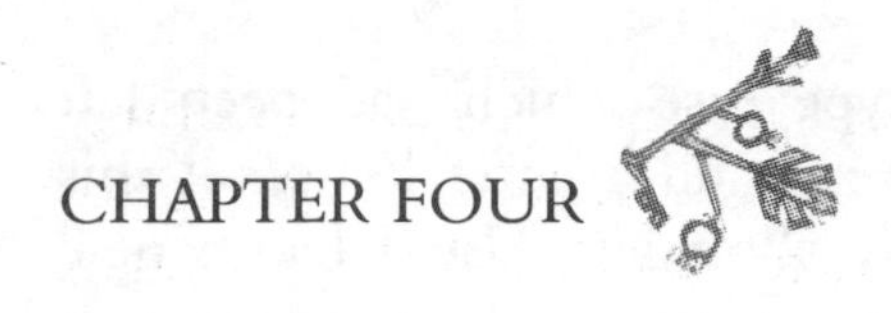

YET what Lucy had said troubled me more than a little. Could it be that a doctrine of love could be twisted so vilely? Or was it simply a story put about by unfriends out of jealousy? Well, if that were so, I could only find out for myself. I am old enough, I thought, to do this. I had been almost a year in Cobham, and now again it was Spring, and the sun hot and cheering in the shop.

I had a few more wordly possessions than I had in hand a year ago. I carried them with me, some in the same basket, but two or three small tools such as are needed for work on a press, as well as the type case which had been left over, some reels of thread and a good knife, all this in a bag slung over my shoulder. Also I had a new kerchief with a small lace edging and, as always, in a thin fold my sea-green ribbons, now a little faded. But it was no more than I could carry and a fine Spring day. I even bought a penny- worth of nuts to crack and eat on my way.

I started on the Portsmouth road, a true highway, but then turned off on to a rough path towards what must be the Diggers' settlement. There were but few footprints and hoof marks that I could see; it was as though they had cut themselves off from the common world. Yet, I thought, they must needs buy some flour or meal and cheese, let alone salt, even sugar and, surely, a few other provisions.

As I came nearer to the Diggers' hill I could see that there was ploughed land and also little huts. I also saw one of these huts pulled down and half-burned. I sat for a time, wondering had I chosen the right path, either the visible or the invisible, but it seemed that now there was no turning back.

Then I saw a small company at work, weeding among the early vegetables on the south slopes, carrots and beets and cabbages. There were also potatoes planted, for they had grown some of these new things which did well enough, each growing four or five roots for the one put in. Beyond were two tethered cows.

I called a good morning across to the weeders. One of them, an oldish man, answered and came over. He stood quietly while I told him I had come out of my sincere sympathy with the Diggers. 'That is well, Sister,' he said. 'Our neighbours in the town of Cobham are not always good friends.' And then he asked, 'Do you have a trade?'

I answered that I knew bakery and also printing and that I was strong. I also told him that my name was Jane Cole, for I wished to forget that Sarah whom I used to be when I was punished and put down with so little hope of any betterment.

'Well then, Jane,' said the man gently, 'we will see how things go. But we will above all trust in the spirit. You know my meaning? Now, put down your basket, come over and help us. I hope you will know a weed from a good plant.'

So I laid my bag and basket on the ground and went over with him to meet these who were now, I thought, my true brothers and sisters. My heart seemed to go faster. They took my hands in theirs and two of the women kissed me. They had their skirts kilted up and the men were bare to the waist and already a little browned from the sun. I left my cloak by the basket and my shoes for good measure, though it was seldom I had gone barefoot out of doors, seeing the dirt of London roads. But I saw that this was the fashion here and indeed the country earth seemed clean and sweet.

We all set to at the weeding; it was a southern

slope, getting all the warmth of the day. They were singing a version of the Psalms, sweet enough. Yet I needed to stand and breathe after a while, for I was not yet used to long stooping. All these months I had been but seldom out of the house, more especially after Mr. Yates's illness. But I struggled on with the field work since I was so deep in interest over my new companions. The seedlings were so small and pretty; we had to be careful.

In a while the work stopped and a pail of water was passed from hand to hand. Then they began to question me. I had made up my mind to say that I was a widow, yet perhaps it was wrong to start them with a lie. In my excuse I might say that this was as I truly felt, for it seemed that my marriage was clouded and gone, as by death.

I told them that I had been with the Levellers – Lilburne, yes, and Mistress Elizabeth – well-known names, even here, and I spoke of our discouragement in London over the Rump Parliament and the breaking down of our thoughts and actions, so that true Levellers were sadly out of heart and courage. I said also that I had read many of their pamphlets and indeed could quote the very words of some of them. That gave my new friends satisfaction; I became aware that not all of them, including many of the women, were readers. But it may be, as I said to myself, that those with little skill in reading may yet have better skill in memory.

After some consultation, one with another, they found me a hut which was empty. Indeed it had a broken roof and no bar on the door. But I could sleep there in safety, they said. I went down to the pool where the women washed themselves and their clothing. The sun was low in the west and I had a great feeling of arrival. Perhaps all would be well.

And so I slept with my anxieties dropping away and was awakened by voices singing what I found as I listened to it, to be a godly song but with some new words, which, I could hear, were cunningly fitted to the needs and hopes of those whom I had now joined. One of the women brought me some thin beer, to drink with the bread which I had, brought with me.

It seemed there was no work for me of the kind where my talents, such as they were, lay, yet I felt that this was deserved chastening sent to show me that I was no better than the rest. I worked in the fields or at washing and wringing blankets, and above all I had the joining together with others in a sweet company of friends in their worship, which was no longer at a set time or place but as the need for it came rising like a fountain from deep down in the very hearts and guts of the men, women and even children – for I remember one six-year-old suddenly taken by the spirit and calling out to God, to the great edification of all of us. And so it went for all the weeks of that spring-time and into the summer.

It became totally clear to me that our way of living, as I had seen it up until now, had been wrongly made up. In Christ there were no rich and poor, no nobles having servants below them. All men and women were created equal and should have an equal share of all the good things with which the Lord has endowed His dearly loved natural world, such as land, water, food, shelter and clothing. The more we could share in good will to one another, the nearer we were to the life of heaven. Indeed this was only one step on from the belief of the Levellers, but there was less politics in it.

Facing us, however, as we could not but be aware, there was anger and enmity, much of it from a man named Platt, calling himself a defender of religion and truly a worse enemy to Mr. Winstanley than Cromwell and all his Generals.

That was to be expected and borne with. What I did neither expect nor welcome was that several of the younger men and boys made advances to me which I thought at first to be risings of the spirit, but now appeared to be altogether another kind of rising; showing me that the ravening wolf which my friend Lucy had warned me of, was indeed here.

The Lord guided me to speak to some of the older women, who in many ways protected me, one in especial by offering me bed space in her small house or hut, a little better than mine. Yet I was uneasy, asking myself how can we truly separate the desire of love, even carnal love, from the love which is of the Lord, of Reason itself, of the Christ which Mr. Winstanley knew and which waits to be born in the heart of every one of us? For there were one or two who argued persuasively that all love carried blessing with it, and indeed there was one in particular who wanted to marry me, and I liked him so well that had I been free we would have married and perhaps my whole life would have been different. I felt a true rising of the spirit towards him, but I knew I must choke it down. Though my marriage was over, it was still there, and now I am glad that this is how it went.

Yet I was plagued with uncertainties. Surely, it was right that there should be marriage and the begetting of children, but more certain still that marriage should be of mutual affection, not from the man alone and not merely a matter of cozening speech, but of the heart? And it warmed and comforted me to see such marriages among both the older people and the young on this rough hill, this land that had been common land, open to all, since before the time of the Normans and their harsh rule. For there was in the same picture, the outspringing of love for each other and also for this land which we worked with our bodies.

Yet for all that it was clear to us that it had only been left common because it was barely fruitful. It was only on the little southern slope that there could be a true garden. There had been little hay for the thin cows and the few sheep to keep them over winter, and the main crops they had tried, wheat and barley, only gave them a few harvest bags. Above all the pair of working horses had to be fed. Thus we had to help our land in every way; we had to make trenches for our own night soil, cover them and then, when they were a trifle rotted down, lay it all into the dug or ploughed land, so that the crops could flourish even a little.

We worked hard and yet merrily, but there was always a risk of depredations from our unfriends in Cobham and elsewhere. On a Saturday there would be prentice lads and any others of like mind who could come over to taunt and harry us a little, perhaps pulling down a hut or breaking our home-made rakes or even milking our poor cows into the ground and laughing at us, who must not let ourselves be provoked into using staffs and forks to drive out our plunderers and teasers.

So, if we were happy in the Lord, we could not be happy over mankind as it showed itself too often. Sometimes, more especially on cold days, for summer was late in coming, I found myself in a kind of despair or non-belief in the goodness of God or indeed doubting that God was truly aware of our suffering. Or was all sent to try us?

I had still a little money and also a yard or two of ribbon, not my sea-green (which I still wore under my bodice, in the stead I would say to myself, of a love letter), but some which old Mr. Yates had given me for May Day and which I had never worn. So I went into Cobham and bought wool, which some of us spun into a coarse kind of thread that could make some notion of stockings to keep off the worst of the weather. I had been ashamed to wear my own stockings when my sisters in the Lord had none. And also we put a new thickness of thatch onto our poor huts.

Not only from those nearby, but from London and beyond, it was becoming clear enough that the Rump Parliament that had been set up was totally against all who thought as we did – not only ourselves, but the Levellers as well – and why? Because this Parliament was made up of gentry and merchants and landowners who were altogether against the notion of equality. They had banished Colonel Lilburne.

What would become of all the London Levellers now, the meetings in the taverns or in the bigger houses, all the talk and the songs and the preaching? Would there be strong compulsion on such as our Mr. Knowles, so that in future he would only speak – as did all too many of the clergy – on patience and trust and a natural law which always put the noblemen, the gentlemen, even the powerful traders and lawyers above the rest of us? No, I thought, this can never be, you cannot turn the clocks backward, and so I would sing to myself some of the Leveller and Digger songs as, I think, more than one of my new friends were doing.

One day came Mr. Winstanley himself, and I wondered could I approach him to ask if there was any possibility of procuring even an old, disused printing press and some paper and ink, so that we could do our own printing and perhaps earn a little to keep us in food and shelter. I had it in mind that with help I might bring a thrown-out press back into working life. But nothing came of this and I put my tools back into the old bag that Mr. Yates had given me once when he was in a cheery mood. At that time our small community were sorely out of courage, so that one or another would slip away, seeking a little comfort and warmth, and our community of true Diggers began to decline.

Yet when Mr. Winstanley preached to us, we all knew ourselves stronger, able to accept any trial which might be laid on us, so that we might become ever stouter and more hungry vessels for the word of the Lord, able to accept any trial which was laid on us, knowing that they were meant to strengthen us, as in a furnace. If a cold wind blew it seemed to matter little when he was speaking to us, so urgent towards the true light were his words.

It seemed, however, that he could make no headway with Cromwell and the Parliament, which could not let us live in peace with our work and our true knowledge of how our lives could be structured into the plan of God's clear intention. This is that the land which is our mother, and all manner of living from the land, should be divided so evenly out that every man or woman should have a fair and equitable share for living peaceably as did Adam and Eve before their Fall. By accomplishing this, we would be going back beyond that Fall, (by which word is surely intended and meant the power of money) and then all mankind would be brothers and sisters and none envious of another, nor ill-wishing to a neighbour. This would be true justice, not the enforced justice of lawyers and magistrates. So I told myself and believed it.

But, while harbouring this belief, I could not make any picture of how it might come to happen. I had known to my hurt and discouragement that men such as my late husband would laugh at these kind of notions, making all manner of dirty tales to turn others against us. To my sorrow I understood how very many in our England were like him, and would never give up a jot of what they counted as their earnings and possessions. Indeed many women would be the same as the men, although I could picture Elizabeth Lilburne as a leader in Digger arguments and doings.

And now came bad news. We heard that the people of Cobham were angry and determined to throw us out, saying that we were giving the whole place a bad name. They were led by Parson Platt, that villainous man forever tormenting us, and following after him other well-off townsmen who were somewhat afraid that our ideas, like a kind of plague, would catch on to the poor of the town, who were many, and could do them harm. They pictured our little Digger community as a disaster and disgrace to the town of Cobham and indeed to England, where already there was too much wild talk and too little business and trading done.

So they came armed with pikes, and even a few guns, and with the town drummers, against us all unarmed unless God could hear and save us. Mr. Winstanley went to the front, calling on the Lord and His messengers, and for a little time we thought there would surely be a miracle, for the sky darkened and there were thunder flashes and lightning that almost spoke for us. But all passed into heavy rain that wet us as we stood and then ran – or at least most of us – before the first rank of the townspeople were on us with sticks and whips, and clawing at the women's dresses and hair. Then they turned to burning our little huts and, worse in a way, they set fire to our haystacks and even the straw bedding. They even broke the few fruit trees we had.

'Oh Jane,' said the woman I shared with, 'this is the end of us!'

Yet not to the hilt. I did not witness it myself, for I was running, but this is how it was. Mr. Winstanley was still in the forefront and crying on the Lord. And it appeared that one of the townmen first pulled at his short beard and then gave him a hard slap on the face, at which he turned his head, showing the other cheek, and the man, a little abashed, backed away, and so did those with him. So there was a calling-off and perhaps a certain shame.

Then came, not the Lord of the manor himself, but a hired lawyer who declared there was rent due and we must pay him. At this some of the Cobham people became angry, saying that if there was money passing it must go to them, for they hated a lawyer more, it seemed, than they hated a Digger.

Then Mr. Winstanley began to speak about money and how it made enemies of those who might have been friends, and some of the crowd became on his side. So now a few began to feel shame at what they had done, more especially seeing the trampled corn. For a little hut can be built again, a little wound can be dressed and will heal, but there is no mending of broken corn.

I was kneeling on the ground at our hut, where they had pulled down the curtain and broken our water jug, when there came a man who had snatched at the bag in which I kept those few tools I had from my work with Mr. Yates, along with my clean linen, and the bag of type. He gave it all back to me. I was indeed obliged, but my cap was awry and my hair had been pulled down and my bodice torn at the neck where someone had grabbed at it, and I did not even answer.

For it appeared that this had happened or that had happened and perhaps there was a cause somewhere; it could be even that we deserved chastisement. This man must somehow be a part of it. I could see that he was trying to speak with me, trying to tell me something. At last it came through. 'Mistress Sarah!' he said, and it shook me to hear my old name used again. 'Listen, listen! I knew old Mr. Yates. I saw thee often. This is no place for you. Come back with me, no, listen!'

I took a step backwards, shaking my head, but he came after me. 'Look,' he said, 'I have no carnal designs upon thee, Sarah. But I know that this is the end of the Diggers, here at least, and you must not stay.'

'No!' I said. 'I cannot desert them now in this great trial which the Lord has dealt on them. I am one with them and surely the anger will at last turn to blessing!' And indeed I was in a way very sure of that.

He said, 'Your Mr. Winstanley is being cared for. We from Cobham had no wish to hurt anyone and we know that he is a good man although he has led you into a kind of morass. Perhaps his time is not yet.'

'But you honour him?' I asked, for there was something in his voice that said that.

'I honour all who have his courage. And yours,' he added, and then, 'But thou canst not stay here.' And when I still did not move, – 'You have the law of England against you now.'

'It is a bad law,' I said. 'It was made by the Normans seeking to keep England in slavery. It is only a law of lawyers!'

'Maybe,' he said. 'I am ill versed in history, but I know where power lies. Where we cannot challenge it we must bow to it and keep on living.'

'Life without faith is nothing!' I tried to stand firm, but he took me by the shoulder and shook me. I think I was crying a little.

He took up my bag with the type box, and my basket. 'Put your cloak round thee, Sarah,' he said. 'Thou must come with me. Later we will hold a discussion on faith.' And after that, as I did not move: 'If you stay here you are in danger of your life. Also of rape.'

At that I began to cry, almost as though it had happened, and I found myself stumbling after him and down thc hill, away from the shouting and screaming and the smell of smoke. And although I had been part of the community of Diggers, although I had joined heartily in the prayers and singing, as well as working in the fields, yet I had made no close friends with man or woman, not even the one who had befriended me, nor yet the man who had asked me to marry him. There was nobody to whom I could wish to say goodbye, unless it was to Mr. Winstanley himself, yct even he I knew mostly through his writings. In some way it was clear to me that I had never truly been one of the Diggers. So what had the Lord in store for me now?

We kept clear of the yelling and the fires. Once I stumbled and fell, but he hauled me up quickly. 'Good,' he said, speaking at me over his shoulder.

Soon we were out of sight, almost out of hearing. 'Where do we go?' I asked in a half-whisper.

'Thou will be safc, Sarah. And both thee and I will concern ourselves with thinking about God's truth.' We went on walking and now we were back on the road and heading, I thought, for Cobham.

I said, 'Sir, I must thank you for your help and courtesy, but I cannot go back to Cobham which is now the City of Destruction.'

I remember that he laughed. 'Sodom, Gomorrah and Cobham,' he said. 'A fine three. But Cobham has evaded the angels and I do not think thou will get a great welcome there. No, Sarah, we shall go to my house. No -' for I was about to say that this would never do. I could not go with him. 'Stop thy fright, Sarah. My aunt will welcome thee.'

What could I do but follow him and those few belongings of my own which he was still carrying? I longed only to lie down and sleep. And this aunt he had spoken of – was he lying? I tightened the cloak round me. It was night by now and we were alone. I began to wonder how he could have seen me in the days when I worked with Mr. Yates. Could he be a writer, a poet perhaps? Mr. Yates's dirty ballads were surely not for him. Or were they? Did he think of me as one of those easy Betsies? No, surely not. And his way of speaking was also a puzzle, for sometimes it was everyone's speech, but then again he would thee and thou me and this, I had heard, was the way of those who called themselves the Friends. Could he be one of these? So in the dark of night, and in sore puzzlement of spirit, I walked on with him and on the outskirts of Cobham we came to his house.

It was a dark house with a heavy door, and I was afraid, but when he knocked a light came into an upper window. Then the door creaked open and there was a woman with a great shawl over her night shirt. 'Whom hast thou brought now?' she said, and looked at me unwelcomingly.

But the man pushed me in and said, 'Now Aunt Bet, she is a poor Digger from the hill, but I know something of her before she took herself there, and what I know is always as good as can be.'

'Thou's thinking that thou's doing God's work for Him, like always,' said this woman, who must, I thought be his aunt, and then to me, 'Come in then.' And she took my hand and gave it a tug.

I was dead tired and might have looked it, and I scarcely keep in my mind how she took me to a small room, a kind of nook off her own, pulled my things off and almost threw me onto the truckle bed under the slope of the roof. And then, before my thoughts could at all unravel, I was taken altogether by sleep.

CHAPTER FIVE

I WOKE to find the day well on and Aunt Bet, as I was to know her, standing over me. She had mended the tear in my bodice, not so neatly as I would have done, but I thanked her heartily. 'Thou will help with the dinner,' she said, 'and I hope thee likes bean soup.' So that was the beginning, the Genesis so to speak, of this new part of my life.

At first I could do nothing but accept what was around me. I understood that those who had plucked me out of my life with the Diggers were themselves godly, but in a way that was hard for me to accept. I started by speaking with a deference which was appropriate for a young woman addressing her hostess and elder, but she cut me short, saying that in this house they spoke truth with no distractions and curlicues, and I must do the same.

From Aunt Bet it was always the plain style, though her nephew, my rescuer, who was more apt to speak without consideration, would often say you rather than thee. I found this plain style, although in a way nearer to the truth, was difficult for me, but I tried earnestly to remember it. He did not use it for his customers unless he knew them well. He was in the wool and cloth trade, as I found out later, and Mr. Yates had printed prices and advertisements for him.

When Sunday came we did not go to any church or set place, and this I understood, but I was somewhat distressed by the unshaped style of their house meetings in which anyone, women as well as men, could and did speak, often lengthily and telling their dreams or certainties. So there was no division of the congregation between preachers and listeners. Even children might be vessels for God's word and others were content to listen to them, even dropping their own work or conversation.

Thus there was no natural order left and it was said formal meetings were a mere invention of mankind and of no importance for the understanding of God's intentions towards His own creatures. Yet this was certainly a kind of levelling and I agreed with it, although with a little difficulty, since it was not pointed directly against General Cromwell or the so-called Parliament.

This congregation of goodmeaning folk called themselves merely Friends, but others were calling them Quakers because of the trances and strange attitudes and performances they might go into, and the strength and violence of their some-time preaching. I looked for leaders or particular speakers for the sake of common courtesy, but this was, so to speak, thrown back at me. I understood that one or two had come from the north of England. I was in a whirl of the spirit, with all truths shown naked in a strong conviction. And in this discipline I now began to understand that spiritiual nakedness was also the way of God.

Yet it seemed to me that the man who had seized on me and marched me off the Diggers' hill, James Kendrick, was less deep in these new notions of God and the relation of people towards God, than Aunt Bet or many of the rest in what I must now consider to be our congregation, though this would not be how they named themselves. James had seen me working at Mr. Yates' press and had wondered at a female doing this kind of work, indeed the most skilled part of it. This had become a kind of warm admiration and interest, and after the death of the old man, he had in time discovered me again on the Diggers' hill. 'I thought I had lost thee, Sarah,' he said and looked at me warmly.

Now I did not know what I should do, for Mr.

Kendrick's interest in me seemed to deepen, though he was not one to snatch a kiss. He was by no means ill-looking and sometimes I wished I could see him in better clothing, at least with a broad collar and some touch of red or gold on his short coat. Yet his hair was well combed and fell sweetly about his shoulders. I began to think that it might be possible that his life and mine might come together, as they had for a moment when he fetched me off the hill. But this could not be.

If only, I thought, I had never set eyes on the man who was my husband. If only I had not obeyed my father so blindly, taking what he had chosen and perhaps now regretted. Sometimes I had evil dreams into which that man, my lawful husband, came. And I could never speak of him. He stood between me and any happiness of the flesh.

Thus I tried never to be alone with James. I stayed with Aunt Bet and listened to her discourse on matters of the spirit, hoping that soon I would be accepted as one of the Friends, as indeed I had been accepted by the Diggers. But at last James came on me rolling pastry in the kitchen and after a few words he asked me – and his voice had gone harsh so that I hardly knew it – did I have any carnal communion with the old man Yates?

'No, no!' I said, for I was somewhat taken aback. 'We were as father and daughter.'

I was truly astonished at his question.

He gave a kind of gasp and said, 'I am glad in the

Lord for thee and now there is nothing to stop me from taking thee as my wife.'

Now I was totally shaken, for, after the first morning, when he was a little anxious over my health, he had never spoken of any measure of relation. And I was the more astonished when he put his arms round me and his mouth against mine and I felt in myself a bodily softening that was new to me and I seemed to cling onto him.

Yet at last I pulled myself away. I remember that I said: 'But sir, you cannot. I have a husband. In London.'

He dropped his arms from round me and half-shouted, 'How? When?' and I was much affrighted and wondered had I done right. He said, 'A husband – Sarah – thou says – ah, bitch!' And he struck me on the cheek. And now Aunt Bet came into the room and I ran to her crying it was no fault of mine, my father had made the marriage. And I had run from it.

'Why?' said Aunt Bet. So I told her all in a hugger-mugger of how it had been and how I had taken the decision and the Lord had been with me. I cried bitterly and held onto Aunt Bet who had tried at first to push me away, but then had listened.

'So!' she said to her nephew. 'This sister of ours is not to be blamed, either by myself or by thee. More like to be pitied.' And she held me in her arms while she spoke to James, saying that now he must go to London and test this story. Above all, neither he nor she were to make judgement until all was known.

Now at first James was in such anger that he could not believe me, but when I had convinced him of the truth of what had happened, I told him the London lane, as also my father's name, but begged him, for the love of God, not to tell them of me in case they snatched me back.

'Yet,' said Aunt Bet, 'it may be thou art called to do a hard thing, to go back and full-face thy parents and this man who is thy husband by law.'

'And by sacrament,' muttered James.

But I cried out, so that the room seemed to shake and it was terrible to me that I might be returned to him and I said I would sooner die. Yet for a short time it seemed to me that one man might betray me to another and all because they were both men, both with that thing between the legs which may be a great comforter but too often is a weapon of the evil one. It was above all sore on me to see that the man who had saved me from the Cobham mob and who had, as I thought, looked on me with great love, yes, of the same kind or intention that Colonel Lilburne had for Elizabeth, was now almost hating me, and that for no fault of mine.

Now Aunt Bet said, 'Wait, let nothing come between ourselves and the inner light.'

So all of us became quiet and waited, but I could not feel the light because of my fear and uncertainty. I could understand well enough how James had thought of me as a clean maid and that now he had felt I was somehow changed and dirtied by what he had heard, although my feeling for him was the same as before he had spoken. And then I began to feel a great guilt suddenly, knowing that although I was a married woman and thus in no position to give or take love from another man, I had yet allowed it to blossom even a trifle between myself and this Mr. James Kendrick, whom, as I now feared, I had truly wished to be allowed to love and obey. And this twisting in my mind of right thinking and wrong behaviour became altogether too much and I could only call in a loud voice for God to help me and then let go into total blind distress and weeping.

Thus I am not certain how it went with the other two, until Aunt Bet had shaken me and was speaking into my face. She said that James was set to go to London and see for himself how things were, but I must tell him in God's truth where he was to look for this husband to whom I must hold myself bound. After that a decision could be made. Had I spoken the truth about where they were?

I said, 'It is the truth but if it is decided to force me back, I shall kill myself.'

Now this was a most wrong thing to say or even to think. But it was not until James had given his promise, would I tell where he would find my husband, as also my mother, but must only let it be told to her that her daughter is alive and safe. I could not now say happy. He agreed, grimly, and with no kind of promise or comfort to me that he would do this, and then he took his hat and cloak, saddled his horse and started off for London. He had business to do there as well.

Now it was borne into me to think deeply about all this and to ask for the necessary judgement on my life and intentions to be made clear to me. The first days Aunt Bet kept me in my room, mostly on my knees, but gave me milk and porridge and sometimes patted me on the shoulder. So it came that in order to think clearly about myself I must also think about the society into which I had come.

They spoke of themselves as Friends, which is indeed a good word, although most were proud of the new nickname, Quakers, saying that they had quaked before God against the evils of mankind. But what does it signify? They were in the same likeness as the Levellers and Diggers, in deep opposition towards bishops and nobles and landlords. Many of them had been parliament soldiers with a great reputation for courage and good sense. Indeed I heard it said that one Quaker soldier was worth four others, since their belief so strengthened them.

But they, too, had come to see that much of what they had supposed themselves to be fighting for, such as liberty of conscience, was not forthcoming. There were still nobles and great landowners standing above the common people, even though they might give assurance to Cromwell and his

Parliament.

When the war ended there was no true distribution of land or riches. There were still tithes to be paid, which last seemed of all things the greatest wrong, since it upheld those who in truth kept from us the spiritual fruit which should have nourished us all. The Quakers struggled, not only against tithes, but against the Universities in which the uppishness of the clergy was born and fostered, and where boys were taught that Latin was better than decent English. So, in many ways, the Quakers had taken over the strength of the Diggers and Levellers. Now I had seen the Diggers discomfited and driven from their hill, although none had been killed and Mr. Winstanley had been taken to a friendly house. But according to all I had heard, the Levellers had been totally put down and some were indeed out of the country. It was sad to think of London without argument. Yet in some ways the Quakers carried it on, though perhaps less in the head and more in the heart. I had been taken to meetings and there was nothing laid down, but one or another would feel a strong conviction and would pour it out, often violently, and with shouting of God's word.

Sometimes it might be straight and convinced argument such as I had heard among the Levellers, on distribution of land or wealth and the wickedness of the grandees, but it was phrased as coming from God's guidance of the heart. For it seemed that all must examine themselves to find what the inner light told them, and this they were bound to make public, since it was not merely their own wordly notion, but from on high.

Again, the meetings might take place anywhere, often in houses, if there was a large room, but also in market places or even in churches, where their voices would overwhelm those of the Minister, whoever he might be, as also of the congregation. This was ill-taken and those who had done it might be accused before magistrates. But the Quakers did not acknowledge any magistrates and would not even pull off their hats in respect. It seemed to me that they had no respect for any persons set in any way above them, and this was perhaps good, but made for rough doings.

So, was I one of them or could I ever be?

It happened when Mr. James Kendrick was away, that Aunt Bet took charge of the business, which she appeared totally capable of doing. The weavers in Cobham and thereabouts brought in their goods which were valued and paid for. Also there might be imports, sometimes very beautiful, so that I found myself longing to dress in one of the silks or fine cottons, but never did I allow a word of this to pass my lips. Once Mr. Havers, who was a bay and say merchant from Colchester, came with two servants and a great pack of the heavy stuff. He too was a Quaker and he spoke of how others had joined and were testifying and of a meeting place they were making. But I had so forgotten my childhood in Colchester that I could not even think in which street it could be.

All those who came to the house, whether members of the Kendrick family or trading visitors, appeared to be totally opposed to the Government and to all that Cromwell and his supporters were doing, but they did not get into argument, least of all with such as me, while Aunt Bet never spoke lightly. She was not angry with me, indeed she was sorry for me, but she did not give me any word of comfort or affection and I went very quietly about my tasks around the house and garden.

There were some thorny gooseberry bushes and I picked carefully, but it seemed that Aunt Bet deliberately put her hand in among the thorns so that they bled and this in a strange way contented her. I never knew for certain whether she had earlier married and lost her husband, or whether she had stayed a spinster. There was never a moment when such questions could be put and answered.

When I had been on the Diggers' hill there had been plenty of talk and much discussion of any news that might come in, either from London or from other communities in Buckinghamshire or from further away still in Middlesex and Bedfordshire, and we comforted ourselves with our own songs and talk of how things could be after the whole of England saw the truth. It was different here. I found myself wondering if there was any way of getting back into the printing trade. Above all I wondered about this man who had, it seemed, watched me for a long time without speaking to me and yet in the end so suddenly proposed marriage. And had I not spoken the truth he would have taken me to himself. And then? If I thought too much about that, I seemed to go into a warm shivering.

He had now been away for several days and I kept asking myself, what had he found? Also I asked myself did I truly wish to be married to him and under his rule. I had followed him from the hill and there was the moment when I was in his arms and softening to him. And not thinking of Robert. Could I trust that moment to tell me my future?

Sometimes I wished I knew what I looked like. It was long enough since I had seen my own face. There was no mirror in Mr. Yates's house, nor yet on the hill where there were so few possessions. But I combed my hair carefully and sometimes I could get a glimpse in a basin of water, if I held it right. My friend Lucy had a little mirror and once or twice I had a peep in it, but could not see my own face as a whole. Aunt Bet had nothing of the kind and if she had I could not have brought myself to ask for it.

At last James came back. I was standing beside Aunt Bet and I felt myself shaking. He looked at me and said, 'I have seen the man you were married to.' I could not tell by his voice what had happened or what he thought. He went on, 'Also the woman who thinks herself his lawful wife and who has a child.'

That shook me. I listened tightly.

'She told me that her husband's first wife had run

away and nothing heard from her, so it was assumed that she was dead.' And now James Kendrick watched me carefully and went on, 'She told me that her husband was a well-bodied man, well thought-of in his trade, a jolly fellow, that he needed a wife, such as herself, and did so well by her that the babe was born not too long after the wedding. A fine strong boy. And she laughed much, and so did the man when he came out of the shop with flour on his hands. Yes, they were merry, the two of them.'

'And so?' I asked.

'I bade them goodbye and I left them,' he said, 'and I went by the other house you spoke of and looked through to the press. I picked up a set of verses as though I might purchase. There was, I suppose, your father, also a boy with light hair.'

'That would be Stephen,' I said, 'but my mother?'

'Yes,' said James. 'I saw her but did not speak with her. She looked a little weary, perhaps with child. I waited by the corner of the house and there came out a little girl, pretty, but with a small scar on her left cheek.'

'That was Doll – my little sister,' and I almost wept.

'Listen, I told the child that she must tell her mother that her big sister was well and in good keeping. I made her repeat what she was to say. She seemed puzzled but when I said the name Sarah she understood. It was the best I could do for thee.'

He came over and kissed me, very gently, on the

forehead.

I stood there, my head in a whirl. 'But if she tells –'

'Yes. Then this other marriage goes. Does thee care?'

'Oh' I said, and now with tears running down. 'What wrong I have done!'

'Yes,' he said, 'and also to me.'

There was no way I could answer. It seemed that I had done him a great wrong and yet I had always wished him well.

From that time on I tried not to be in his way and Aunt Bet helped me over this. She would often send me out on errands when he was in the house, so that he would not see me. I could not even guess what James had in mind for me and whether he still cared for me or even intended to marry me, only I felt I should somehow find myself work elsewhere. But how?

I went sometimes to the meetings with them, but some way the preaching and crying out did not touch me as it did Aunt Bet and her companions. The only time we seemed to be together was when one of the great preachers from the north came into Cobham and burst into the anglican church, defying them to stop him. It was somehow in the same voice as those I had heard in London among the Levellers, although the words were different.

Sometimes I asked myself did the Quakers fully accept the beliefs of the Diggers and the Levellers on such things as the redistribution of wealth and the dividing up of land so that all could share, which would be the end of all oppressions and hatreds? It seemed such things would be made clear by the inner voice and those who heard it must be eager to bring it about. But they did not put into practice the setting up of protest and pressure upon lawmakers and Members of this un-admirable Rump Parliament, nor the writing and publishing of pamphlets.

For most of my life I had thought, at first a little, but then more, about justice, about rich and poor. My mother told me that Jesus was poor, not even with a roof against the rain. We Levellers wanted justice, so that England should be no more a land of rich and poor. The Diggers went further, showing that there could be no true justice until the land itself belonged to everyone – or to nobody, as in Paradise before the Fall – and surely that was right, only hard to come by. And it would happen on earth and especially in England – the chosen country – in God's good time. But it seemed that the inner voice did not always tell the Quakers this, indeed they had judged the Diggers as being wild and foolish. Because of this James Kendrick had been on the side of the Cobham people when they said the Diggers must go, and only against them when they took to violence. And now? What was the inner light telling him?

Not, I thought, to care that some had more money than others, though he was for fair prices, which is better than nought, but was it enough? And if he gave all his goods away, who would pay the weavers for their work? And how had the inner light spoken to him of me? Not, I hoped, in the bitterness of his first words. Indeed he now always spoke gently to me. What, then, were his intentions?

So I was much troubled and there was no-one to whom I could speak. Winter had come and there were cold winds and sharp frosts. I had no warm clothes, but Aunt Bet gave me a skirt and bodice of good woollen stuff and after that an old cloak of hers, so I did everything I could to help in the house and with running of errands.

Once I came upon some of my old friends from the Diggers, but they were sadly put down. They told me that Mr. Winstanley was well and had written a poem about the righteous law and changing the heart of man. I would have been very happy to have a copy of this, but had no money to buy one, and I could not ask, as even a godly poem would have seemed wrong to the Friends if it did not carry their own strict and particular message.

They told me that the Levellers and Ranters had been totally put down in London. There had been heavy censorship; all unauthorised presses were being searched out. I heard that the Rump Parliament had perhaps taken a step towards justice for the people of England: much law which had only been in Latin was now turned into decent English, so that anyone who was in question might understand why he had been charged. Yet it was hard to make sense of what was happening, or how

General Cromwell was moving, for he would make some great statement which seemed to show he was favouring the cause of justice, as I at least saw it, but then again he would swing like a weathercock.

It seemed that we might soon be at war with Holland. This was mightily important for the cloth trade, which had long been too closely in Dutch hands. But it made me anxious to know of Colonel Lilburne, who was, I understood, in Holland to escape the capital judgement against him in England. I wished to my bones that I could be with Elizabeth once more.

Then happened one thing that pleased me much. I remember it as if it had all passed not earlier than yesterday.

I had carried over a parcel of fine cloth to a customer's house, and who did I meet but my old friend Lucy. We stood together under a great tree which sheltered us a little,and had a free and loving conference, speaking easily about our hopes and intentions. She was near the end of her time as prentice and was considering the setting-up of a business by herself and her fellow prentice on the glove-making side, whose father had promised him the business.

'And then my own father has arranged for my marriage,' she said. 'Oh dearie me, I had not thought to marry so young, but he has the prettiest hair and his blue eyes... and you, Sarah, how did you fare with those terrible Diggers?'

So I told her, not all, but as much as would satisfy her; and then it came to her asking me about the young master where I stayed, whom she knew by repute.

'I cannot tell where his thoughts or inclinations are going,' I said. 'He will follow his inner light.'

'Which you should set the taper to,' said Lucy, and gave my arm a little pinch. That was the moment when it came to me for sure and certain, that this was not what the Lord had truly in store for me. There was another road, once I could see it and set myself upon it.

CHAPTER SIX

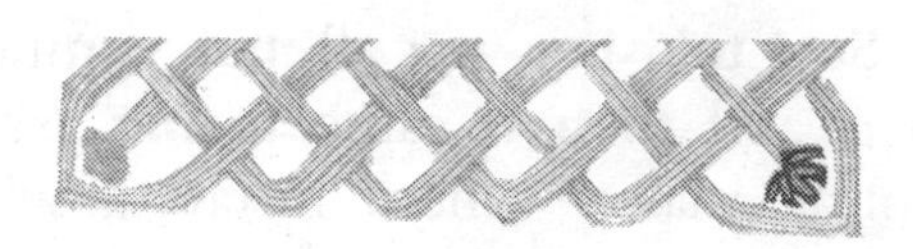

IT WAS a cold winter. I did not like to come too near the kitchen fire unless it was to stir the pot and Aunt Bet had her own notions of what we should eat. But at least she allowed me to make the bread and there was a good bread-oven at the side. I wished I could see a way to find work outside the house. There was no printer now in Cobham, and poor Mr. Yates's old press was rusting away in a shed, but even had it been shining new this was no time for printing. All was now in strict control by the Government and the Stationers.

There was talking in plenty of the state of England, but I could hear only such tigs and tags as appeared in conversation between Aunt Bet and Mr. James or any of their guests at the meetings, where there might be crying out and shouting and talk of justice wronged and the works of Satan, or else of the intentions and great victories of God and his true followers. But there were not many clear accounts of what had been happening in London, or in any other parts of the great world beyond the streets of Cobham.

What I liked best at this time was carrying goods from the warehouse at the back of the house. I learned how to pack and tie and not a little about the cloth itself. They understood that I could be trusted to go straight to the customers' houses or the tailors, or it might be across to the inn at the market corner where customers sometimes stayed.

Aunt Bet lent me a great grey cloak, under which I could carry a heavy basket or parcel. I had this cloak over my bed at night to keep out the cold. Yet the surest way to keep that cold at bay was the fiery preaching, with leaping and shouting from the congregation, which, although all was in the Lord's name, could amost have been dancing. And I might find myself pulled this way and that, and there were times when I wished it would finish, both with the Lord's approval, and at the same time with a warm arm round me.

Yet I knew, too well I knew, that this was but a base part of me that made such a picturing and I would step away, often enough crying like a baby. And I wished to my heart that I could be with my mother and my little sisters. But that could never be, and never again would I meet with Elizabeth Lilburne, who, for me, must be as dead as my dead Robert. And now it was almost the second year since I had left my home, first for Cobham, then for the Diggers' hill, and I wished God would grant me some true resting place.

The days began to lengthen out but it was still bitter cold, and the March gales cutting through the streets. I was sent with a heavy parcel of cloth – it was a good brown, not too dark – to a customer called, as I heard the name, Mr. Rainer. I took the roll under my arm, with the cloak over it. I was wearing high clogs to keep my stockinged feet out of the wet where the snow was melted. So I came to the inn and asked for Mr. Kendrick's customer. He came, a more soldierly man than I had expected, and younger.

'I have brought your cloth, Mr. Rainer,' I said, not dropping a curtsy, as I had been told often enough that this was wrong, even to a good customer, and the knee should only bend to the Lord.

He frowned and said, 'The name is Rainsborough.'

'I am sorry, sir,' I said and then I could not but ask, 'Perhaps, sir, you are related to Colonel Rainsborough?'

'He looked at me hard, 'You know of him?'

'Indeed, yes,' I said, and then, 'His very words at the Putney talks, I know them by heart.'

'I am his younger brother William,' said the man. 'But you are, I think, a Quaker?'

I answered, 'Sir, I am one of a Quaker household, but truly I am at heart a Leveller.'

'Let us sit down,' he said and called rather sharply for ale and cakes. I got to my feet, for I felt that I had already gone too far, but he took me by the hand. 'Stay a little,' he said. 'It is good to hear that name again. But you are in the employment of the Quakers?'

'They have been most good-hearted towards me,' I said, 'and I must not stay.'

I remember that he smiled and I asked myself, had he the same face and features as his brother? I felt that I was doing no wrong and would be returning soon.

He questioned me a little and I answered, as I hoped, with truth and modesty. But when I said that I had also worked at printing he took me up, and questioned what I knew of it and where I had learned and practised the trade.

If now my mind can go back to that meeting, and so indeed it often docs, I seem to recollect that there was a table between us which had been much used and scrubbed over, yet still smelt a little of spilled beer. I drank but a mouthful and nibbled at the cakes which were none of the best. I had my back to the window; he faced it and I tried to see a likeness between this man and the picture of his brother which had been on a pamphlet covering the Putney debate between the Army of the Revolution and those, including the Generals, who could not or would not accept the peoples' will. But the woodcut showing the army leaders was ill drawn.

All the while I was wondering, first, how long could I loiter here and with what excuses, but also what was truly in this man's mind. At last I said I must go back to my duties, or my master – for such I called Mr. James – would question me.

He said, 'You shall hear further from me,' and he signed a paper for the sale of the cloth, which I had taken out and spread on the table, and said he would pay within the month.

He came with me to the door and then fastened the buckle of my cloak with his own hands. One finger touched my neck for a small moment but yet I could go on feeling it. And he?

I walked my way back with a strange kind of elation which I could not understand and indeed only wished to keep. I turned over in my mind all that he had told me; that he was sailing for the Americas and was now collecting his cargo. All goods from England sold at great profit out there, as I could well understand.

He had said that after the war was over and the mourning, first for his elder brother and then for his other brother Henry, he could not settle, for he could not bear to see the pulling down of those who wore the seagreen ribbons. In this mood he had gone to America – Maryland, it was called – in partnership with an older man. They had grown tobacco and things had gone well enough for the space of two years. But then came terrible fevers and sickness, his partner had died, and he decided to come back to England.

'I sold all our slaves,' he said and this gave me a jerk in my mind.

'Slaves?'

'Yes, but maybe this is wrong. I have thought it out a little since then. Also I bought a smaller piece of land which I fancied, further up the river, well drained and timbered. The trees are most beautiful...'

I saw him looking away from me, smiling.

Then he went on, half to himself and yet I kept in mind his very words. 'There is no house there. Not yet. But soon. There could then be – yes – a small press. There is none in all that country and no Stationers' Hall to forbid it, nor any licence needed.'

And he looked hard at me and smiled. He intended to set sail as soon as the March gales were past. And before that – but already I had a swirling in my mind.

I told Aunt Bet that I had been delayed at the inn before I could see our customer, who was well pleased with the cloth and would pay soon. He understood that one did not barter with the Friends; he knew them of old.

Later that day I was sent on another errand but I cannot now bring to mind over what or to whom. I questioned myself, yes, on my knees in my cold little room, hoping for guidance from the inner light, for I could not but ask whether there was not a new way opening itself towards me, though as yet uncertain. This man had most certainly said that among his cargo there would be a small printing press, for there were plenty on the market now that so many printers were under threat from the Government and the Stationers' control. He had said that he believed the new Americas or whatever-they-might-be-called, would find themselves wishing for books or pamphlets, even for songs.

No, he had not directly asked me to come with him as a printer, but yet I could see that he had it in his mind. Perhaps, I thought, he might look on me as a small gift from the Almighty to help him on his way, in so far as it was a virtuous and noble direction. Was it possible that I had become even the smallest part of the divine intention which covers all mankind? I stayed long on my knees in the cold, wondering about this man and the Americas. How far was it truly? Further than the Low Countries of Europe. Further than the Indies and the silk which I had touched once or twice. Further than the great sea itself.

Now time went on, the gales blew themselves out, it was the end of this bad winter. Mr. James had been to London again on business and when he came in and dropped his cloak, he had a strange look.

He said to me, 'The man who was your husband is dead. I understand that he had a vile tumour. The doctors drenched and cut him, but he died. Is buried. His widow keeps the shop.'

And he looked at me in a kind of burning way and I did not at all know how to answer this. What road was he thinking to take? I only said in a small voice that I must go to my room and say a prayer.

'Do that,' he said, and seemed pleased.

So I was on my knees but I could not get even a touch of the Lord's will or blessing. I knelt on the hard boards and I tried to turn my mind on a godly course; in a while Aunt Bet came in and touched me on the shoulder.

'Thou are a good lass,' she said. 'Dry thy tears and come to us. We will not ask you yet for what is in thy heart.'

So we sat down to supper, but I could not eat much, though Aunt Bet pressed me. Suddenly I was in tears again and went to my room and again knelt beside my bed asking with all my strength for an answer. I blew the light out and crept under the blanket, waiting for some sound. I did not know what I wished or what I expected. Had I interpreted what Mr. Rainsborough intended towards me? Sometimes I cried quietly. But the inner light would not shine on me and suddenly I was asleep.

No more was said and I was glad of it. But a few days later Mr. James said, 'Thou will now have had time to think a little. Shall I take thee to see thy mother? And the little sister?'

'My mother!' I cried. 'But –' and I did not know how to go on.

But he did, '...and tell her,' he said, 'that her eldest daughter is considering a better marriage.' And he smiled down at me.

I felt myself all at cross purposes. I said, 'And the woman who thought herself a wife – and bore him a child – must she be told?'

'The law might say that she has no right to inherit,' he said, for he had not understood what I was trying to put into words. 'Yes, it could truly be that she has no right to inherit. Yes indeed, it could be that the shop is now yours or your father's!'

'No!' I broke him off. 'I would not wish for any of it.'

'Yet,' he said, 'your parents might think –'

But I kept on shaking my head and at last I ran out of the room and again I could not stop my tears or my sore uncertainties. If only I had felt again that little warmth which had come to me earlier when Mr. James had asked me to marry him, I would have felt a little happy and as though my life might be on the right course. But that had died away.

After a while Aunt Bet came with a bitter potion which she had made and I had to swallow. She told me that both of them understood my agitation and would ask nothing of me until I was back in my right mind. I was thankful for this. When I said that this was occasion for deep and earnest thought and the coming of the inner light, Aunt Bet seemed to think the better of me.

Yet I felt I was in some way cheating, setting my own will against what might be God's, for surely Mr. James was a truly godly man and well esteemed by the Friends, as well as being in a comfortable situation as regards his wool and clothing business. My parents would welcome him. I also knew that I was deeply indebted to the kindness both of the man himself, and his aunt, to a poor, battered, penniless girl, for that was all I had been after the break-up of the Diggers. Who else could have acted so well by me?

Yet, could I be sure that it was the Lord's expectation and will that I should become the obedient and dutiful wife of Mr. James? Or had that moment passed? Could it truly be that I was free to make some choice? Suddenly I was wondering whether Aunt Bet, in her time, had been at a cross-road of the heart and, if so, was it God's will which had solved it. But I also knew that this was something I would never be told.

I longed very much to see my mother and the little ones. I would also have been most happy to know how my father and his printing business had gone and whether the Leveller group had kept at all together. Had Mr. Knowles been forced to change his preaching? How had the Overtons fared, or Catherine Hadley? Above all, Elizabeth Lilburne! I would even have liked to see Stephen. But not with

Mr. James beside me, claiming me. For that would be the price.

So what did I now think of him? Had the softness towards him that I had felt at one time come back, or was it no longer allowed to me? Twice I went to large meetings of the Friends, listening, trying to find a prayer which would echo the puzzles in my mind. But always at the end of my prayer the inner light flickered and left me. All that came into my mind was that now the month was up and Mr. Rainsborough would be coming to pay for his cloth. And if he did not?

CHAPTER SEVEN

BUT SO it came about. There he was at our door with his man beside him, both in heavy coats – army coats, I thought – even although the winter cold was over. He did not speak to me, other than to include my name in his general greeting, yet he gave a small twist to his lips, which seemed to have meaning for me. He went out to the warehouse with Mr. James, who later came back in good heart: Mr. Rainsborough had ordered more cloth, saying he could certainly market it well in the Americas, to whichever port he sailed.

Later, when the cloth was cut and I had put on

my cloak to carry it over, Mr. James asked, 'Is it not too heavy?'

I said no, no, I would wish to be of help. Indeed it was heavy, but I tried to step away jauntily, and yet all the same I felt the kindness in Mr. James' voice, which in turn gave me a touch of guilt, but not the old warm feeling I had for him in that moment before he called me bitch.

So I came to the inn by the market place. I had put my knot of sea-green ribbons on my shoulder, but a little hidden. When we met Mr. Rainsborough saw them at once and smiled.

He said, 'Let us sit together once more, Mistress Sarah.' He seemed to handle my name sweetly, so that I could not if I would nay-say him.

He told me that the ship was ready in Bristol harbour; they would be sailing as soon as the weather was totally settled. He spoke of winds and directions and I was in a maze, not understanding but aware that there was something else that he had to say. At last it became clear to me that the ship would be bound for this Maryland in the great America. I heard the name Chesapeake, but it meant nothing to me. He said there was good land for tobacco to be grown as well as flax and sweet potato and the crops we all know. There were already many small farmers and the beginnings of a town, but as yet few in commerce or business, and few women folk.

'But, sir,' I said, 'does that give a public of readers

large enough for the printing press you spoke of?'

He smiled very sweetly and said, 'Your printing press. Waiting on you, Sarah. Well packed. Perhaps I myself will write that which can no longer be printed in this poor country which has so cruelly nipped the bud of freedom.'

'I would like above all to print that,' I said.

'So,' he said, 'you are sailing with me? And perhaps never coming back?'

I could not answer. I crumbled one of those poor inn cakes in my hand. I thought of my mother and Doll and the others. But I could only speak with them again if I went with Mr. James and as his wife to be. Mr. Rainsborough was speaking again. Casting my eyes down, I saw that his shoe buckles were plain, but silver certainly.

He said, 'I cannot see that England will ever turn to equality of Government.'

Well I knew that he was thinking of his brother and all that the Army had hoped for, but Cromwell had denied them.

He went on, 'But it might happen elsewhere. You, Sarah, your ribbons,' and he put his fingers very lightly on my ribbons, on my shoulder. He went on. 'The Diggers also. Did you think about equality?'

'About justice,' I said, 'for the poor.' But all I had in my mind was his hand on my shoulder.

He said, 'The hard field work in the Americas is mostly done either by slaves or by indentured servants, who have bound themselves for four to six or seven years, as payment for their passage, and are, so to say, sold by the Captain of the ship. I think there is a better way. Yet these are almost all small farms and the owners have to work as hard as the rest. Could not that turn into a kind of justice, or at least equality?'

'Yes,' I said, 'and I know field work from my days on the hill.'

'I had to learn it,' he said, 'for I was bred up too softly. Now I can hoe-up planting mounds with the best. And I think I could undertake the building of a house – and a place for the press.'

'I can also make excellent bread for sale,' I said, and then, before I could even check myself, 'You might marry me, William Rainsborough, for the use I can give you.' And then I buried my face in my hands.

He pulled them away gently, 'We should indeed marry before we sail,' he said, and then, speaking with great earnestness, 'You are a free woman. Would you wish that?'

I turned to the Inner Light and it said Yes, yes. I thought of what I owed to Mr. James, but now the small warmth I had for him was quite gone. I was deeply grateful to Aunt Bet, but that was all. Yet I could not tell them of my intention. They would most certainly stop me, perhaps even by force. They would see me as a lost sheep leaving the fold, and would consider it their duty to bring me back. And now, I said to myself, it is time for me again to make my own decision.

Gravely I said that this was my wish and intention and then we spoke about the goods he was taking and how he was arranging for this cargo to be brought into Bristol to go on board the ship. The small press would be well packed and there would be a great bale of paper. I asked should I bring my type, but he said no, there was plenty. Yet in the end I brought a small packet, including my best capitals. The rest I had to leave.

Before we had finished talking his man John came in and looked at me hard. Mr. Rainsborough turned to him and said 'She is coming.' And the man said, 'Good,' and then took my hand and said 'We will care for you.'

The three of us spoke about the goods which must certainly be taken on the ship. Suddenly Mr. Rainsborough turned to me and asked had I ever ridden pillion on the back of a horse, but I had to say no. 'Well,' he said, 'I shall need to hire a cart for the goods which I must, for sure, take. I wish I could offer you a grand carriage.' That made me laugh and suddenly he said, 'I have never seen you so full of cheer. But I warn you, love, it will be hard travelling.' And suddenly he threw his arms round me.

The days passed. The good weather settled after that hard winter. I had never seen the sea, but I knew well how it came pushing up the Thames, fingering into the mouth of the Fleet and going back and away carrying all the dirt of London, the night-soil carts emptying themselves into the lapping water. Somewhere beyond, among great waves, was Leviathan and doubtless other monsters.

As for the Americas, I could not guess. It was not clear to me what was taking shape in London and elsewhere. But it was sadly certain that we had lost all our hopes of justice and some measure of brotherly help towards those who had lost all during the war and the poor soldiers with their wooden legs and scarred faces, yes, and the desolate widows and mothers. Had General Cromwell forgotten the days when he had brought us all together?

Mr. Rainsborough had gone back to his own house and small lands which he must sell with all his furnishings and belongings, keeping only what would sell best in America. He must sell his riding horses before we sailed, keeping only his dog. His man, John Perkins, had also sold all he had; he was an old soldier who had, like so many, lost almost all his small possessions during the war and was hopeful of a new life, although, like me, he had never seen the sea which surrounds this great island which had been our home. Here, it seemed to me, was a good friend.

I tried always to be busy, and put off the time when I would ride to London with Mr. James, even feigning a stomach sickness and swallowing the black draughts which Aunt Bet forced on me. I was glad indeed when Mr. James went away on a matter of business and stayed for a good number of days.

Sometimes I thought, Is it possible that I am in a dream and Mr. Rainsborough is only a shadow that I have imagined? Yet when I went on my knees to pray and only to think of God's mercy and reality, I felt a certainty that this time all would be well. I spent many hours in writing a letter to leave for Aunt Bet, thanking both her and Mr. James, begging their forgiveness and asking them to pray for me. I wrote it more than once and at the end I yet could not say all.

And then came the old soldier, John Perkins, to the door. When I opened he said, 'Get ready. Church Alley – you know it? One hour.'

'Oh,' I said. 'Oh, so soon?'

'One hour,' he said again. 'We have a covered cart. They will not follow you. Do you understand?'

'Yes,' I said and pushed him out and went to the bundle I had half packed. I would not take the good cloak which Aunt Bet had left me, only my old, worn cloak which I had snatched up when I was pulled away from the hill. I had few possessions, but I had faith that what I was about to do was right.

Then I was climbing into the covered cart, quickly, hoping that no-one had seen. Except on a Church service time there were few about the Alley; easy to leave a small cartload there. I had just a glimpse of Mr. Rainsborough, my Will, up on his horse. John Perkins pulled down a flap of the cover, hiding me, and suddenly we were on the move.

It was hard going. I felt I would be jolted out of

my bones. There were chests with hard knobs and corners, bundles, farm tools, including a plowshare – I knew a body could be fitted to it; this had been done on Cobham hill. There were also carpenters' tools, including a great saw, some wine and beer, a whole box of books, a rolled feather mattress and what was clearly a press, well packed. I also saw a large and heavy parcel which I thought might be paper. My press. And so?

That evening we came to an inn. There was an upper room, tolerably clean. A bed, not very wide. So what? Mr. Rainsborough said, 'Give me one blanket. One pillow. Over by the window. The bed is yours.'

'But, sir,' I said, and then, 'Mr. Rainsborough – William – is this right?'

'We are not yet married,' he said. 'Go you to bed. Or say a prayer first and I will join it.'

So I knelt and said a prayer, remembering what Mr. Winstanley had said about Christ in the sons and daughters, and at the end I vowed to God and deeply did I mean it, that I would forever love and cherish this man who had been granted to me. I lay for a while thinking very softly about William Raisnborough and how our life together might be. For a moment I had a dreadful fear that somehow I might be discovered and pulled away from him. But I put that aside.

So it went for the five days and nights it took us from Cobham to Bristol. There again he took me to an inn, but this time left early in the morning. When he came back he said, 'We shall be married at three o'clock and the Captain of the ship on which we sail will witness it.' And then, 'Ar't glad, Sarah?' But I could only bury myself in his arms.

Before we sailed there were a few days for us in Bristol, which is a marvellously rich place, with its narrow valley going up from the harbour, and people crowding and moving everywhere. There were smells I did not know, especially from the bales of tobacco, but these were mostly from the southern Americas, and so were the packs of sugar. There were some other sights, among them some black men who were being sold as slaves. I asked William if that was right and he said no.

They were different from the bonded men he had spoken of and now he was somewhat ashamed that he had ever been a slave owner. 'And,' he said, 'I will buy two bonded men at the end of the voyage. I shall have watched them and seen what metal they are made of, and so will thou watch, Sarah, for they must serve you as well. But they will not be slaves.'

He would have enough money, he said, to stock the land he had bought two years before. He said he would have to build a house, for there was not yet any building on it. 'But you, I am sure, will be as willing to make camp as any soldier.' He would also enquire in the town as to the printing prospects.

'But first,' I said, 'you must write,' and he laughed and kissed me.

The very last day before we sailed, he gave me a small gold chain and a cross of garnets, which, he told me, had belonged to his mother, who was dead. But he also bought me a gown, not heavy and not silk, which I would not have wished for, but of a fine, light Indian cloth, cream and strawberry coloured, with little sprigs. It was indeed far from taking my mind back to the gown I had worn that long time back, for my sad London wedding. But of a sudden, I was taken with weeping and yet under it I was deeply happy and looking, as it were, across the seas.

We had a small cabin on this ship which was so full of ropes and sails and oars and every kind of thing that I had never seen before. There was little space for most of our goods, which were piled into the cabin, and his small pretty dog on the top of it. We were high up on the ship, and there was one small window, but if the waves were big, we must make the shutters fast over it.

John Perkins had a kind of kennel at the other side of the ship into which he crawled, but he ate with us.

The Captain of the ship was, I thought, a decent man, and very wise in his craft or profession, and his wife a kindly woman; they had one small child with them. Another had died. Every Sunday of that long sailing William shared a bottle of his wine with them. There were a few others who had paid their way over on the ship, but I did not speak to them much. There were no women. The men seemed to be young and from well-doing families, apt to boast of what they would do in America.

The sea went on and on and it was a great day when fish were caught and a better day still when we saw the first sea birds flying round us. Before that I had wondered if there could truly be an end to it. We ate salt meat, cheese, heavy puddings and hard bread or porridge without milk. The water began to smell foul about the middle of the voyage, but there was always small ale. Sometimes I felt, if only I could have an apple, even a bruised one! The Captain's wife had a bag of raisins and sometimes she gave us a few, but they were mostly for her little girl, and there was also a babe in arms.

After some weeks of sailing, we put in to an island called, I think, Bermudas, very busy and noisy, where our water butts were washed out and filled again. Indeed the last water had been too foul for drinking and the sun was coming hotly onto us. But here we got fresh food and indeed went on shore and bought fruit and a kind of sweetmeat. Here the great crop was sugar and there was a smell of it everywhere. But we were told that their tobacco was less easy to market than that of the great Americas, where we were bound.

Then we sailed again knowing that, God willing, the worst part of our voyaging was over. Yet the great waves knocked the ship up and down. We became used to the sailors shouting and the noise of the sails and rope-ends tapping and scratching, and always the wind somewhere in the rigging. I had brought needles and thread and did what I could, and also I read the books which my husband had brought with him, and some of which was poetry. Sometimes I thought of the lady called Deborah who had set me so kindly on my way of travel and escape, and whose husband had been a poet. And all the time I had the feeling that God had forgiven me my trespasses and I was His child.

William and his man John watched the indentured men, who slept below, on straw, and certainly ate worse than we did. Some of them grew sores, but the Captain said these would mend when they got ashore. Too many of them had brought strong drink with them, and there might be noises of shouting and bad, even blasphemous, singing.

Which of them should come into our household? Before the end, half of them were ill in some way, mostly with sores, but sometimes with sharp fevers. Two died and the bodies were dropped into the sea. But there were decent men among them, not shouting and swearing with the drinkers, and my Will and his John – often with me – would watch a little and speak about them and what skills would be of most use. Some were country folk, others had a trade but had wandered over England, finding no work and their savings gone, so this ship was now their best hope. There was a watchmaker, and even a wigmaker, from as far as Newcastle; there were skilled ploughmen who could manage both horses and oxen, a miller, a hedger and ditcher. Many of them had come to London where, the old songs said, the streets were paved with gold, but instead they starved.

We decided that we needed a builder or joiner who was used to making wooden walls, for there is no lack of timber, and a good ploughman who could also be put to digging and fencing, and who had some knowledge of cattle and swine, which Will told me, ran half wild and were most used for meat. Above all, our need was for men who would be willing to work well and deserve our trust if they had good treatment.

After the first two or three weeks these men formed themselves into groups or, as it were, families. I could hear that some of them were praying or singing psalms or holy songs. And several times we heard some of the old Leveller songs and I wondered if they had been true Levellers or only engaged by a catchy tune. William and I began to go about them a little, and I bandaged up the arm of a man who had torn it against some of the ship's gear which was slipping on a day when the wind was high and the sails filled and drove us on, but the great waves knocked the ship up and down.

William and John spoke to some of the men who seemed most likely, asking as to their trade and experience, and how many years they would serve as indentured servants and what would they expect as freedom money. It was a strange kind of bargaining, but a way of finding out what kind of person might be inside a body that was like as not to be dirty and battered.

Mostly, on that part of the journey, the sun was high, the wind pushing us on to the Americas, but not to the southern part which had been claimed by the Papist Spaniards.

And then a man shouted from up the mast and it seemed that land was in sight, though it took long enough before the Captain was certain of where we were and turned the ship a little, so that we could make the mouth of the Chesapeake river. I clung to the rail, watching. It was totally against my expectations, but my Will pointed out the places he knew. For, although named as a river, it was so large that, if we saw one coast, we were hard put to see the other. There were islands that seemed part of the land itself and as we moved cautiously up, with many of the sails furled, small boats came after us, offering for sale cakes and trinkets and asking for news of England and Germany and Holland, often enough of Cromwell, some even asking if we had yet got back a king, which angered me not a little.

At last we reached the harbour at Providence, where is the office of the man with whom Will had been dealing. It was strange to be on solid ground, no more rocking. We came to an inn and I waited there while Will went to the man's office. John Perkins stood guard over me, for there were some who stared and would have questioned me. But the most part were stiff-looking and wore the kind of dress that the old Puritans favoured, for I believe it was they who founded this town. Then came my Will back, saying all was in order but he must get horses and a cart, and also see to buying the two indentured men which he and John had decided on. I could stay a few days with the wife of the Captain, which I was indeed happy to do and to escape from the eyeing of strangers and questioners.

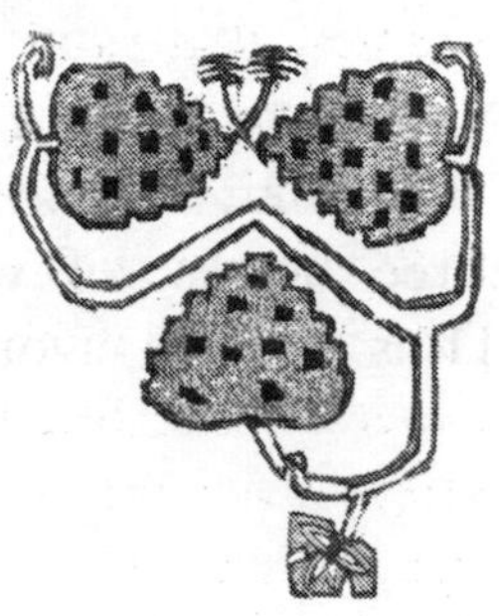

CHAPTER EIGHT

WILL had done business over the two men, and had also bought a small cart and three horses, of which there were a fair number. Thus he had avoided the expense and indeed the uncertainty and danger of taking his own across the seas, although I know it had been a sorry parting. He rode and his other two horses were harnessed to the cart. John and the two indentured men walked beside it, one at a time taking a turn on top of the load which was all of gear and tools needed for the farm and a great piece of tent cloth to give them shelter at the beginning. I wished very much to go with them, but

on his promise that he would be back before the week was up, I obeyed as a good wife should, and the Captain's wife said jokingly that she would see that I did not stray.

I went about with her a little, looking at the town and wondering at the folk we saw and also the goods for sale, often at such high prices that I found myself laughing, for example a few loaves in a baker's shop. Yet fruit and some victuals, especially salt pork, was cheap enough. I saw for the second time some black men, who, my companion said, were slaves.

Turning over in mind the thought of the one I had seen in Bristol, I asked myself whether all who were born with black skins were caught in a destination of slavery and it seemed to me that this could never be God's choice. Doubtless the people of England had been near slavery after the Norman tyranny which indeed partly went on until my own days, but now that was over, although wc must still look that it did not come back.

'No,' I said to myself. 'There is a tangle somewhere and we must see through it, for it is not simple poverty. Plenty of poor working folk have I seen in London, but this slavery means something else.'

Then I cast my mind back to that first talk with Will, when he told me about his doings two years back, with a tobacco farm worked mostly by slaves, and how he had started to become uneasy, aware in his mind that this was in some way wrong. So I wondered about these black men who were said to be slaves, but who, I thought, were no worse clothed than the rest of the working folk. I must have stared unbecomingly, for one of them laughed and kissed his hand to me, so that I felt myself blushing.

There were some rich-clad men riding good horses and once a lady riding who wore a handsome laced coat.

'These are the great landlords,' said my friend, 'coming in for the Sabbath, but not a word! For they are Papists or near enough, as are most of the great families who hold wordly power here, such as magistrates and councillors. But they let the decent, God-fearing rest of us alone, so you need not fear.'

I tried to find out more, for I was shocked to think this fair country could be under Papist rule. Surely this could only bring disaster in the end, for the Lord is not mocked. When I spoke of this to the Captain's wife, she laughed and showed me two small wood-built churches, not very different in their building, but one a papist place.

I peeped in at the door, and I saw the dreadful idols and sniffed the kind of smoke they use. There were lights inside, but I did not linger, for I understood that they have no care for justice nor the true ways of the Lord. Yet it seemed that here they flourished like rats in a kitchen, those at the top giving places to others of the same persuasion, so that it was unwise to speak against them. And yet, I thought afterwards they, like the black slaves, are human beings, and perhaps God has some purpose even for them.

'Go your own ways,' said the Captain's wife, 'and if you do not choose to anger them, they will not hurt you nor stop you from your own way of serving God.'

'Indeed,' I said, 'they cannot do that, but they will never have me worshipping with them.'

'Ah Sarah!' said she. 'There is only one God that is worshipped by all in Maryland and that is tobacco.' And indeed it was a matter for laughter that both she and I liked so little this stinking herb which was to be our livelihood in the new world.

Instead of tobacco we ate strawberries, which pleased me mightily, all the more that I was now certain and praising God that I was at last with child. There were also large fresh oysters, more for a penny than ever in London. There were many friends of the Captain, who came to our rooms to greet us. It seemed that there were as yet few women making the crossing. And I longed for Will to come back to me.

At last my Will did come back, saying that I must learn to ride pillion which, indeed, I was eager to do, so I got up for my first lesson and held onto his belt with my eyes shut, and tried a good smile at the end of it!

There seemed to have been some trouble over the boundaries, but this was now put to rights. Indeed beyond our estate was a tangle of thick forest and bushes, a no-mans-land. Will told me that it was late in the season for most planting, but one of his neighbours would give him enough young tobacco plants for perhaps half an acre, so he had set his two indentured men to dig the ground with the heavy iron hoes and make up the small ridges or hummocks for planting the seedlings. But as soon as that was finished they were to start on the house which had been laid out. Meanwhile, he said, we had only a shelter of branches and must live like Adam and Eve, and how would that suit me?

I told him I would do better than Eve and eat only wholesome fruits, and we packed my gear into the saddlebags, my gown that he had given me carefully wrapped, and again I was up on the pillion, while he told me more of what he and his men had been doing. I felt the horse moving under me while I wondered at the crowding of new sights, for sometimes we would be deep among noble trees or else splashing through mud and trickles of water coming down into the great river, and often there would be a strange and pretty sort of bird or squirrel. Then we came to our new home and John Perkins coming to help me off and give me a good welcome. The planting was finished and they had begun on levelling the ground for the house and cutting the great corner posts from some of the many trees which were all around.

The next thing was to plant walls of scantlings from smaller, easier trees, and get them well bedded. After that came riven boards from the great trees.

One of the men, Thomas Ubbley, had good understanding of all this. The next week there was filling-in with clay and at last a roof of shingles, but meanwhile we lived in our camp of branches and tent cloth, with all our cooking on a fire that must be fed constantly with small wood.

I liked it well enough and, while the men were at work, I could sometimes go walking alone, and this way I took myself to every corner of the property. I came on several great nut trees and also wild fruit, which I brought back in my apron heaped full, much to the pleasure of all. I also tried out a few herbs, one of them much like an onion, others like parsley or sage. I felt that indeed there was a whisper of the Garden of Eden, and I knew that Will and I would come to love it dearly.

Thomas Ubbley had good skill and had brought his own tools with him. At first the two men were somewhat afraid and uncertain, seeing that I was their mistress. But on the first Sabbath, Will called for a meeting for prayer and after it he spoke to them, reminding them that Thomas was to work for three years, James Tyler for four, and for food, shelter and clothing only; yet he would always respect their rights as fellow men. They agreed and understood and did not, I think, feel hard done by. We ate together, after asking blessing for our meal, and I saw that they had as much as any of us. This way all went busily and I began to feel myself able, not only to face the day, but to face the years that the Lord has allotted to me in this new country, among those whom we had never seen before, but whom I now believe we have led into what is becoming almost a family.

The house, now that it is finished as far as we can work on it until perhaps next year, is made up of one good-sized hall with a room partitioned out of it at one end and at the other the fire and chimney. For this John Perkins had to take the cart and buy bricks for the hearth and chimney. He and Thomas built in a cross bar so that I can hang up my pots, but I fear the cooking will be poor enough and mostly stew with always a backing of a kind of flour from the Indian corn which is good enough for cooking, but will no more make bread than a fish will fly. Perhaps next year we might grow a little wheat, but only if it can be fenced, and there is so much else to do.

Will has bought some cattle, including two cows near to calving. I have never milked a cow but he says I will come to it easily, and indeed it will be a pleasure to have milk again. He has also bought a small herd of swine, for this is the main meat. They run wild among the trees, eating whatever falls to the ground. And now I have a few laying hens and hope soon for a brood of chicks. Meanwhile the press stands in the corner of the inner room, waiting.

The main thing is to get the land dug and to weed carefully in the small planting of tobacco, for this will be all that we shall have to live on for another year. It seems now that there must be more digging than ploughing, but maybe in time we might grow other field crops, though always this tobacco must come to be the staple. But at least my Will affirms that he will never take to it! There are those who chew it or smoke it until they stink.

I spoke to Will of my disquiet, hearing that many of those in high places of this part of the Americas were certainly Papists, but he said that as yet there was no telling of how this government truly was. There is a strong system of laws here, much as in England, but here we are not yet certain even of the names of those said to be above us; for want of this knowledge we are surely free to act as God's people, in so far as we can. We think, at least, that justice is in the hands of juries, rather than judges, and that is surely good.

Will tells me that he has heard of yet another way of thinking, by those who believe that the end of the world as we know it, is just at hand and that all will be changed in the twinkling of an eye and angels will descend and end all earthly government. This seems strange to me, but there is so much strangeness here. I have seen, but not close, several of the Indians; I wondered if they were truly people like ourselves and if so what is God's intention towards them. I could not certainly decide which were men and which women.

Yet by now our two so-to-say servants are truly familiar to me. Both are in their middle years and had once made a fair living in England until things went badly. James Tyler seems to be handy with the cattle, and finds them easily if they are strayed. I had at first an awkwardness speaking to him as James, (for I still ask myself if that other of the same name has forgiven me). Thomas had come to London looking for building work but found that there were too many others already there. So I tell him, hoping it will give him cheer, that now he has built a small house and soon, perhaps, it will be a bigger one. But we must see how it stands for the winter cold. I hear that the winters here come hard. James had, as a boy, been for a short spell with the army, but had taken little to it, although he remembered the names of commanders.

So things have gone on and so much to do every day that I can scarce remember now what thing happened first and I am more than a little uncertain of the names of such other folk who came to visit, not always for good reasons. For some were surely at our door to spy upon what we are doing or having a notion to do, and sometimes indeed speaking to me in ways which angered Will and which I did not wish to understand.

Yet others were truly friends and there is talk of building a small church, although for now we go back to Providence whenever there is a Sabbath on which we can be spared and the horses are in good shape. But I am anxious that Will should not spend too much, even of our pennies, for we shall need them all even if we get a good price for the tobacco.

But here I must tell of the strangest droll thing that happened and that did indeed cost us more than pennies, though they were well-spent. I was riding pillion with Will, with a saddle bag either side. I needed salt and hoped for pepper, and also sugar from the cane plantations to the south of us. And just as we got to the market square came a big black man rushing over, caught at the bridle and shouted something I could not rightly hear up at us.

Will reined in angrily but then looked down at the man and said, 'Why, Toby!' and 'What is it? What ails?'

He reached back and patted my knee, for I was afeared since indeed the man looked strange and ragged, bleeding a little from under one eye. Yet the little dog, which we had with us, jumped up on the man as though he knew him well.

Will leaned over, speaking to the black man Toby and there were words I did not know and both were angry. Quickly Will told me that the man to whom he had sold the slaves had mistreated them with beatings and kickings and most of all this fellow Toby, who, Will had told me, had been a great worker, but obstinate and standing up for himself. He had clashed with his new master, been sorely beaten – as indeed I could see – and chained at night in the dogs' kennel.

He still held to the saddle while Will turned to me and said low, 'He begs me to buy him back. What must I do, love?'

I tried to understand, but it seemed above all strange. 'To our house?' I asked. 'A black slave?'

He nodded and said, 'A fellow man. Who has had justice denied to him.'

I said, 'You will do as the Lord tells you.'

Out of the saddle Will bent over, asked where his master was, and then to me, 'Sweet, go you to the inn. Wait there.' He handed me down, then trotted off, the big black man running beside him. I waited in the garden of the inn, in a mood of great uncertainty. I tried to pray for guidance, but then the woman of the house came out and sat with me, whether I would or no, and soon enough got talking on my lying-in, with too much said about accidents and difficulties.

Then, after what seemed like long hours, Will came back with the man, who had at least washed the blood off his face and put on a shirt that was rough stuff but clean.

'Now,' said Will, 'we have a new friend.'

And the man went down on one knee and kissed the hem of my skirt. I could only whisper a welcome for underneath I was a little frighted and wondering, Could the black come off on me? He came with us when we bought the salt and sugar and walked briskly beside the horse, running when she trotted, and I asked myself what would our own men say.

And well I might ask, for at first the two bonded men were totally against poor Toby, and they would not agree to having him eat or sleep with them and this the man seemed to accept. But I had been thinking deeply about this matter of slavery and could it be right, so when Thomas and James were so stubborn, I would not have it. Indeed I was angered, more than a woman should be who is carrying a child.

'If this is the way of it,' I said, 'You can eat and sleep by yourselves, but those of us that care for justice will eat with this poor slave who has been worse done by than any of you!'

Will began to pat my arm to quiet me, but yet half agreeing. Then John Perkins said, 'Well I have seen worse. At least he is no Papist.'

The poor wretch Toby could see how things were. He moved cautiously towards John, saying he could sleep out, he was not afraid, nor likely to run away from a good master, and the small dog knew him. And then John came over and said he did not care if it was the devil himself, so long as there was a Rainsborough at the head of the table. It was the two indentured men, especially James, who proved difficult. In the end, I believe they came round to some kind of understanding, not through good principles, but because Toby was a great worker who understood the work better perhaps than my Will who had watched others but never handled tobacco himself until now and is sometimes a little clumsy in the handling.

Toby knew what was needed and started on it as soon as it was light. For now the tobacco plants were well up and the flowering sprigs must be cut off and the leaves singled out so that there must not be more than twelve left on each plant. Toby would simply look at one of our tobacco plants and judge which leaves must go without counting, yet as comfortably at the right limit as those who had taken time to count.

Later he was the one to whisper to John that it was time to cut the stalks, before the leaves had spotted and shrivelled. Indeed it sometimes seemed to me that he was a blessing sent by the Lord and I have altogether stopped thinking that his black fingers could leave a mark on my linen. I patted his hand once when I gave him his porridge, and it was no different.

So now the men began to look to him for guidance on the crop. For example, he knows exactly how the leaves should be laid for drying and the others seem content enough to follow where he leads.

I find myself making meals for five hungry men and it is not always easy unless there is enough meat. Will has shot deer and so also has John Perkins, as well as a kind of large wild fowl which was truly good eating. So far we have sold the deer skins, but I have in mind to cure and make cloaks for winter from the next one they shoot.

I must also try to cut meat to salt down or smoke. I believe Thomas Ubbley will help me over this. He has quite a turn for the small things I have asked him to do around the house. And, just an hour ago, he tells me that he has left a wife and child; she is back with her parents but at the end of his time he hopes to bring her over, and then – he shakes his head, but I am glad he told me. At least we can help him to write and send over a letter.

We have been so altogether concerned for the field work and the beasts that until the other day we had not even loosed the cords and ceilings from some bits of the baggage. One evening Will came in. He had been cutting and splitting fence posts and torn his shirt at the shoulder. He said he thought he had a leather jerkin somewhere and began to root about in a great bundle, still corded, that had been in our cabin on the ship. He found his jerkin, but said it was winter wear, he would sooner go bare-shouldered while I mended his shirt, and then he pulled out something wrapped that clinked together and this was two small silver candle-sticks. I cried out with pleasure, but he was somewhat abashed.

'They could have bought another saw!' he said.

But when they saw them standing on our rough-made table, the four men all seemed happy and proud, and James Tyler shook his head and said, 'I had never thought to be that near table silver!' He touched it with his finger tip.

But I have not yet made candles. This is yet another task, though a happy one. I would wish soon to have a small garden dug by the house; even planting so late we might get cabbage, turnips, parsnips and the like. It would all help, and seeds are to be had. There was one little rose bush in our London garden and I think there are wild roses here.

John Perkins came in but now, and tells us he has seen a black bear. If he can shoot it we may have a bear skin rug for the floor; hard earth may do well enough now, but not so well in winter. But he and Thomas, and now James joining them, and all together bidding me take care, not to go too far from the house. Toby does not speak, but I think he has the same thought. It is as though I am some kind of treasure. They are making me a cradle, but I am not to know yet.

So the days are full and at night Will has me very quietly in his arms and we talk about what we intend, he and I together, with the bed curtains drawn round us, so that we do not even hear John or Thomas snoring. The others sleep quietly and the little dog sleeps at the foot of our bed.

When he was last in town Will was thinking of plans for next year, as soon as the first ships come in. Then we will set out all the news in type, not only from England, but from Holland and Germany and perhaps Scotland. That, he is sure, will be most profitable. It will certainly be the first news to be printed, perhaps in all Maryland. Meanwhile we have also a plan of a popular broadsheet, with a song or two, and even, as he told me, something he hopes to write himself. But he must be circumspect and not, for example, taunt the Papists. One day I put a small bunch of flowers onto my press. Neither of the indentured men had ever seen one and Toby bent a knee to it.

Up to now there is truly too much to concern us in our common living. Will has to get us a new chamber pot, which saves me from going out in the night. So much is left to be done and we look to next year as full of small triumphs over our difficulties, that is if we deserve them, and still set our hearts on justice and freedom.

Only yesterday James Tyler was complaining that his hands were blistered from the digging. I know how it is, he hates to dig, wants to be with the beasts. But it has to be done and these heavy hoes tear up the ground fast enough. I was a little angry, but Will spoke with him, saying that his present condition was for a few years only, then he will get his freedom money, which is twenty pounds and a suit of clothes and new shoes, and after that he will be free either to work for wages or – says Will – to join up with the Indians. Meanwhile he must work like a man. Also I found some scraps of cloth which he could tie round his hands.

Thomas is going at it well. So of course is Toby. Perhaps I may teach them some of the Diggers' songs. They were writ for a different kind of company, but yet they might give a little cheer to these ones. Today I took out my sea-green ribbons; they are a trifle faded, but I have a notion that John Perkins at least will know them. We have very little money left, partly because of what Will paid for Toby, which was not within his calculations, yet I am most glad of it, seeing the man now. Meanwhile I have a good store of the cobs of the Indian corn ready to soak and pound, and much else. Once the tobacco crop is away – and I am a little sick of the smell it has – I will set Toby to the pounding, which is becoming a trifle hard on me. They tell me this corn is very sweet to eat when it is young. There are so many tastes and smells that one can never be tired.

There was one thing which caused me anxiety. It had been cruel dry and hot weather for too long and we feared for our crop. I saw Toby look at the sky, then fall into muttering and make that sign which the Papists use of a cross on the body which is surely a kind of image making and a relic of the days when England was enslaved by the Roman Papists. So I spoke to Will and he to Toby, though it was hard to make him understand this measure of wrong doing. I thought that one stroke of the whip if this happened again would be enough to warn Toby of this folly, the more so that we have explained to him that his late master whom he bitterly hated was himself a Papist or almost one. Will tells me, also, that it can be that a slave may become an indentured man and in the end come to total freedom and if all goes well we can consider this for our Toby.

So we are well set on our road and hope for blessing. When Will goes to town, sometimes I go with him and I am getting to be easy on the pillion. But sometimes I stay at home. At night I wrap myself in his great cloak which still smells of the sea. And of him. But also I can put my trust into this family that we have made and that I hope is growing into a kind of fellowship, counting on justice and the words of God. I have thought a little about my lying-in and have laid aside and washed well some soft pieces of linen and wool. How will it be? I have scarcely met with any woman here. The Captain's wife is long back in Bristol, though I trust we will meet again next year if God wills it.

So I mostly put my trust in the Lord. If I bear a boy we shall call him for his uncle, so that there will again be a Thomas Rainborough. But if it is a girl I will call her Elizabeth, after my dear Elizabeth Lilburne and the Levellers, of whom in a certain way I am still part.

OTHER TITLES FROM BALNAIN BOOKS INCLUDE

POVERTY CASTLE *Robin Jenkins*

pbk £7.95 — The happiness of an ideal family in rural Argyll is tempered inexorably by events and the socialism of industrial Glasgow as this new 'novel within a novel' of contrasts and irony subtly unfolds.

A BIT OF CRACK AND CAR CULTURE *Bess Ross*

photographs by Gunnie Moberg. pbk £7.95 — This highly acclaimed 'village of stories' sings with the life of a Ross-shire shoreline community.

FISH-HOOSES *Stanley Robertson*

illustrated by Eric Ritchie. pbk £6.95 — Scottish best-seller by master story-teller who shares tales and experiences from 35 years he worked in the fish-trade.

LETTERS TO GYPSY *George Mackay Brown*

illustrated by Simon Fraser. hardback £12.95 — An amusing and unusual collection of wry letters written by this celebrated Orcadian author to a Very Special Cat named GYPSY

IN SYMPHONY AUSTERE *Richard Frere*

illustrated by Eric Ritchie. pbk £5.95 — Well known author and man of the hills.

for a complete catalogue contact the publishers:

Balnain Books, Druim House, Lochloy Road, Nairn IV12 5LF
Scotland